TH
ERNEST T

Ernest Thompson Seton was born in South Shields, County Durham, in 1860, the son of a shipbuilder. When he was still a young child his family emigrated to Canada. He studied at the Ontario School of Art and at the Royal Academy in London. In the late 1880s he travelled to New Mexico and there started on his life-long work as a writer and illustrator of books about animals. By the time he was forty he had received almost every honour that North America could bestow on a naturalist, and at the time of his death in 1946 his writing had earned him a permanent position in the affections of those who enjoy sympathetic but realistic accounts of life in the wild.

Further information about Ernest Thompson Seton will be found in Richard Adams's Introduction to this book. A full account of his life and work is available in John G. Samson's *The Worlds of Ernest Thompson Seton* (New York, 1976).

The stories in this collection have been chosen from the following books by Ernest Thompson Seton:

'Raggylug, The Story of a Cottontail Rabbit', 'Lobo, The King of Currumpaw', 'The Springfield Fox', and 'Silver-spot, The Story of a Crow' from *Wild Animals I Have Known*.

'Badlands Billy, The Wolf that Won', 'Little Warhorse, The History of a Jack-rabbit', and 'The Slum Cat' from *Animal Heroes*.

'A Street Troubadour, Being the Adventures of a Cock Sparrow', and 'The Kangaroo Rat' from *Lives of the Hunted*.

'The Well-meaning Skunk' from *Wild Animals at Home*.

The cover painting is by Ernest Thompson Seton and shows the front runners in a pack of wolves in full cry. Wolves fascinated Seton – to such an extent that he incorporated a wolf footprint into his signature.

THE BEST OF

Ernest Thompson Seton

Selected and introduced by

RICHARD ADAMS

FONTANA PAPERBACKS

This selection first published by
Fontana Paperbacks 1982

Set in 10 on 12pt Lasercomp Plantin
Made and printed in Great Britain by
William Collins Sons & Co. Ltd, Glasgow

Contents

Introduction

Born in 1920, I spent my early years in the very thick of the 'Christopher Robin' period. In fact, Christopher Robin and I must have had very similar childhoods. Our parents came from much the same social level and lived in similar rural areas of southern England. We were at prep. schools which played each other, and I remember him batting in a cricket match when we were both thirteen.

At this time the general tendency (though only among the middle class, I think) was for children to be regarded by their elders as beautiful, innocent little creatures, passing through a golden age of infancy which ought not to be spoilt by the intrusion of anything harsh or cruel. Up to a point there may have been some sense in this, but nevertheless it was an incomplete idea. In particular it gave rise to a kind of soft-centred, 'sugar candy' school of writing for children. Gone, of course – gone centuries before – were the children of Tudor and Stuart times, dressed like little adults, often treated with severity, over-disciplined and made to learn too much too soon. Gone, too – or at any rate, long grown-up now – were the Victorian children (like Alice) brought up in an atmosphere of kindly but serious-minded religious moralism. During the first three decades of this century there was a certain irresponsibility in the attitude of many middle-class English parents towards childhood. Wishing their children to be happy and to feel secure, they too often tried to exclude altogether from their lives any suspicion that pain, mortality, risk and loss are unavoidable in the human situation. The truth about childbirth, of course, was unmentionable. (Nowadays most seven-year-olds seem to be pretty well-briefed.) But so, very often, was anything at all connected with pain or death. For instance, you might be told that the cat had 'gone away'. Two days later you learnt from the gardener that it had been run over. Or you might be told that an injection, or the dentist, wasn't going to hurt. Then you discovered, with a feeling of betrayal, that they did. It is always a mistake to tell lies to children, and that includes what lawyers call *suppressio veri* and *suggestio falsi*. Children are shrewd. They discern that they are being deceived and this lowers their confidence and can set up strain and anxiety, which get transferred to other areas of life.

The survival for over fifty years of *When We Were Very Young* and the Pooh books is proof of their charm and quality, but they need – they always did need – counter-balancing with tougher, more truthful and realistic stuff. And in this they were not alone. The 'sugar candy' school of writing – and by that I mean anything that contrives to suggest that the world, or at any rate the reader, is ultimately secure – includes several other well-known works, some of them still going strong on their very real merits, such as *Peter Pan* (1904), *The Wind in the Willows* (1908), the girls' school stories of Angela Brazil, and the verse of Rose Fyleman, which first appeared in 1917. Perhaps a stanza from Miss Fyleman's poem, 'A Fairy Went A-Marketing', will exemplify, better than further words, just what was wrong (and what I felt as a child was wrong).

A fairy went a-marketing –
She bought a winter gown
All stitched about with gossamer
And lined with thistledown.
She wore it all the afternoon
With prancing and delight,
Then gave it to a little frog
To keep him warm at night.

Now there were counter-balances, of course – more truthful and demanding stuff – appearing during the thirty years of which I am speaking, and much of that is still going strong, too. For example, Walter de la Mare's *Songs of Childhood* appeared in 1902, and *Peacock Pie* in 1913. Hilaire Belloc's *Cautionary Tales for Children* was first published in 1907. Eleanor Farjeon was off the mark by 1916, and on a different, but very welcome, level, the first 'William' book (*Just William*) by Richmal Crompton appeared in 1922. (William is beginning to 'date' now, and modern children cannot be expected to realize that the real secret of his enormous success was precisely that he provided a good, 'bolshy' counter-balance to Christopher Robin and Rose Fyleman.) One must not forget, also, that a steady flow of Beatrix Potter continued from 1902 to 1922.

When I was a child in the late 'twenties and early 'thirties, there was one prose writer above all others who comforted and sustained me and made me feel more grown-up, principally because, quite apart from his sheer charm and readability, I felt – indeed, I knew – that he was telling me the truth, with no holds barred. This was Ernest Thompson Seton. There was no sugar candy here. The stories were not trivial, like the Pooh stories. On the contrary, they were about survival and death, and usually appallingly real. Though they were often very sad, moving you to tears, there was nothing revoltingly or mind-preyingly cruel about them (like Mr Squeers in *Nicholas Nickleby*, or Simon Legree in *Uncle Tom's Cabin*). When Molly Cottontail, the mother rabbit in 'Raggylug', went through the ice and drowned; when Krag, the Kootenay ram, was at last shot by the hunter Scotty, I wept – but I also knew that the author had respected me as a fellow human being, and treated me as a potential adult by telling me the truth. A wise, knowledgeable, entertaining, grown-up friend who could be trusted to tell you the truth – what a find! I read every one of his books I could lay my hands on, and many of them I still have in the splendid original formats, with their (often frightening) photogravure full-plate pictures and beautiful marginal drawings, all by Seton himself. Like Beatrix Potter, he illustrated his own books and he did it more than well.

In point of fact Ernest Thompson Seton, whom I am extolling as the ideal counter-balance to the sentimental literature too often thought best for children during my childhood, had begun his long career as a naturalist and writer much earlier. He was born in 1860 in South Shields, County Durham, where his father was a shipbuilder. The family name was actually Thompson, and it was not until 1901 that Ernest Seton Thompson changed his name (as transatlantic emigrants not infrequently do) becoming Ernest Thompson Seton. The reason appears to have been that he had never been very fond of his father, who was rather a stern man and in Seton's view often unkind to his mother. Seton was fond of his mother (she bore no less than ten sons, and the couple adopted a daughter – *faute de mieux*?) and tended to idealize women all his life. I think it likely that his family background may have had a good deal to do with his life-long sympathy with the hunted and with under-dogs and victims in general. Another reason for his change of name was probably family pride. It was the correct name. The Setons are, of course, an old and honourable Scottish family, by hereditary right armour-bearers to the kings of Scotland (see, for example, *Macbeth*, Act V, Scene 3). After the '45, in which they were involved, some of them came south and changed their name.

The Thompson family emigrated to Canada during the eighteen-sixties and Seton, having become Canadian, retained that nationality until becoming American in 1930 at the advanced age of seventy. In 1878–9 he won the Gold Medal at the Ontario School of Art and within the year returned to England. In December 1880, after a hard preliminary struggle during the previous year, he was awarded a seven-year scholarship at the Royal Academy School of Painting and Sculpture. (Amongst other benefits was free admission to the London Zoo, of which he took full advantage.)

He spent part of the 'nineties on a cattle ranch in New Mexico, and here began his life-long career as a writer and illustrator of books about wild creatures. In 1896 he married a wealthy American girl, Grace Gallatin. Their daughter, who was to become the novelist Anya Seton, was born in 1904. At this period of his life, on account of his wife's wealth and social connections, he spent a good deal of time in New York and also had dwellings in New Jersey and Connecticut. He was on friendly terms with several of the best-known scientists and naturalists of that time. He also knew Teddy Roosevelt; and 'Buffalo Bill' Cody. Towards the end of his life he and his first wife divorced and at the age of seventy-five, having left the east and moved to Santa Fé, New Mexico, he married his secretary, Julia Buttree. Their adopted daughter, Beulah, still lives in his very large Santa Fé home. Seton died in 1946.

He was immensely prolific and between 1896 and 1945 produced no less than forty-two books. The great majority of these are the kind of animal story book for which he became well-known, but there are some interesting exceptions. For example, his first book was *Studies in the Art Anatomy of Animals* (1896) and in 1910 he published *The Boy Scouts of America Official Manual*. Some regard him as the founder of the Boy Scout movement in America (as well as of the American Camp Fire Girls' movement), since he started, as early as 1902, an organization he called 'The Woodcraft Indians'. He corresponded with Baden-Powell over the formation of the Boy Scout movement, and Baden-Powell always acknowledged his debt to Seton's detailed knowledge of the Red Indians and of nature.

It is worth emphasizing that at the time when Seton began to champion the Red Indians, writing with first-hand knowledge and passionate admiration about their virtues and traditional skills, they were still 'baddies' to most white Americans. 'Two Little Savages' (1903) and 'Rolf in the Woods' (1911) are based on Indian woodcraft and lore. General George Custer, of the US Cavalry, a notorious 'Indian-hater', was killed at the battle of Little Big Horn, Montana, in 1876 (when Seton was sixteen) while leading part of a military expedition against the Sioux. For many years Custer remained an undisputed American national hero. Seton, throughout his life, maintained openly his opposition to the veneration of Custer and did all he could to get recognition, justice and fair play for the Indians, whom he regarded as the most misunderstood, exploited and ill-used racial minority in the world. In 1937, at the age of seventy-seven, he travelled to the burial place of Chief Sitting Bull of the Sioux (against whom, *inter alios*, Custer had been fighting in 1876 and who was captured and killed by American soldiers in 1890) in order to be photographed, hat in hand, beside the grave.

But indeed he loved all fierce, untamed minorities, whether human or animal, faced with a losing battle to preserve ways of life threatened by 'civilized' man. His chief loves were wolves, coyotes and bears. (He incorporated a wolf's footprint into his signature.) While in New Mexico during the 'nineties he found himself required to play a part in hunting and trapping a pack of timber wolves which was playing havoc with the cattle on the ranch. (See

'Lobo, The King of Currumpaw'.) He once said that he could never forget how the great wolf, Lobo, after being taken by means of a female decoy, had refused to eat and simply pined to death in captivity.

To what extent should Ernest Thompson Seton be held to be a writer of anthropomorphic fantasy – stories in which animals are made to think and talk like human beings and are therefore, to some extent, falsified? Anthropomorphic fantasy is a very old – perhaps the oldest – type of storytelling, its roots going back into the dim and distant past. Such stories play a large part, for instance, in the folklore of the Australian aborigines, the most primitive people known to us today, and are to be found among the folk-tales of all nations. In its primitive form this type of story, as I suppose, fulfils two functions. The first is a magical one. The story purports to explain and account for some curious feature of an animal – the giraffe's long neck or the camel's hump – often with reference to the animal's dealings with a god or spirit. But secondly, such stories can also take the form of social satire. The animals represent different types of human being and the hearers are amused by the teller's wit, which makes a crafty rabbit, a stubborn, slow tortoise, a foolish monkey and so on, correspond to people within their own experience. What is of interest is that as civilization has advanced, this type of story has not died out, as one might expect, but has maintained its attraction and adapted itself to keep up with different kinds of consumer demand. Chaucer knew the *genre* and used it in *The Canterbury Tales*. Six hundred years later George Orwell's *Animal Farm* has become one of the most widely read books published during the twentieth century.

To-day anthropomorphic fantasy has, as it were, separated out into different kinds and might be likened to a spectrum. Beyond one end of this spectrum, as a matter of fact, there lies a kind of 'infra-red'; that is, the 'straight', realistic animal story in which there is no anthropomorphism at all. The best-known examples of this are Henry Williamson's *Tarka the Otter* and *Salar the Salmon*. At the opposite end is found *The Wind in the Willows*, in which the animals are to all intents and purposes human beings except in name. (Toad has a butler and drives a car, while Rat can read and write and use pistols.) With Beatrix Potter, we have a strong element of mild but shrewd social satire which, in *The Pie and the Patty-Pan* and *Ginger and Pickles*, rises to affinity with Jane Austen herself. Kipling's formula might be said to lie somewhere in the middle of the spectrum. While attributing to Kaa, Bagheera, Baloo and the Seeonee wolves motives and intelligence which their real counterparts could not possess, none the less he never makes them do anything which would actually be physically impossible to real animals. (This, incidentally, is also the formula for *Watership Down*.)

Thompson Seton should be placed on the outer edge of the 'realist' end of this spectrum. He is writing in earnest, from personal experience, about real animals and purporting to attribute to his characters nothing but what he knows they felt and did in reality. Yet he contrives to anthropomorphize them to the extent that he makes us think of and sympathize with them – to feel emotional about them – *as if they were* human beings. In this respect he exhibits more warmth than Henry Williamson, who is concerned to emphasize the difference between animals and humans; to describe the stony indifference of Nature to extremes of suffering and animals as creatures responding, like computers, to stimuli. When Tarka is hunted to death at the end of the book, Williamson obviously feels compassion, but is careful only to imply it obliquely. Seton, by contrast, is much warmer and more openly emotional.

He is even prepared to allow his creatures snatches of simple dialogue. 'Let me show you how,' says the mother Grizzly to her cubs, when they are learning how to lick up ants. 'That's right,' says his mother to Raggylug the rabbit, 'always keep the runways clear; you will need them often enough.' (And there follows a considerable dialogue between Raggylug and his mother.) In other passages, however, Seton merely puts into words the meaning of an animal's cry. In 'The Trail of the Sandhill Stag', the prairie wolf 'gave a gentle, dog-like "Woof, woof", a sort of "Oho! so you have come to it at last."' Lobo gives 'a long, plaintive wail' for his mate. '"Blanca! Blanca!" he seemed to call.'

This technique is certainly anthropomorphic, but it is hardly fantasy. The truth is that Seton did not really distinguish, in his emotions, between animals and human beings (except that he preferred animals), regarding both, primarily, as different species inhabiting the earth. His men, for the most part, are not villains. They are just men, as the wolves are just wolves. Such anthropomorphism as he went in for gave expression to this view, and was intended, as it were, to translate the animal's actual feelings and cries, without falsifying them, into terms readily comprehensible by human beings. I suggest that this is as good as, if not better than, explanation. He never departed from natural realism, and, as I said before, he never pulled his punches. You get the truth. If you don't like it, whether you are seven or seventy-seven, better stick to Pooh and Piglet.

How did he write? He wrote well. Here is an example of his straight, unemotional description.

Old Olifant's Swamp was a rough, brambly tract of second-growth woods, with a marshy pond and a stream through the middle. A few ragged remnants of the old forest still stood in it and a few of the still older trunks were lying about as dead logs in the brushwood. The land about the pond was of that willow-grown, sedgy kind that cats and horses avoid, but that cattle do not fear. The drier zones were overgrown with briers and young trees. The outermost belt of all, that next the fields, was of thrifty, gummy-trunked young pines whose living needles in air and dead ones on earth offer so delicious an odour to the nostrils of the passer-by, and so deadly a breath to those seedlings that would compete with them for the worthless waste they grow on.

And here is an emotional passage, from the closing pages of 'Krag, the Kootenay Ram'.

The White Wind rose high that night, and hissed and wailed about Scotty's shanty. Ordinarily the stranger might not have noticed it; but once or twice there came in over the door a long *snoof* that jarred the latch and rustled violently the drapery of the head. Scotty glanced at his friend with a wild, scared look. No need for a word; the stranger's face was white.

In the morning it was snowing, but the stranger went his way. All that day the White Wind blew, and the snow came down harder and harder. Deeper and deeper it piled on everything. All the smaller peaks were rounded off with snow and all the hollows of the higher ridges levelled. Still it came down, not drifting, but piling up, heavy, soft, adhesive – all day long, deeper, heavier, rounder. As night came on, the Chinook blew yet harder. It skipped from peak to peak like a living thing – no puff of air, but a living thing, as Greek and Indian both alike have taught, a being who creates, then loves and guards its own. It came like a mighty goddess, like an angry angel with a bugle-horn, with a dreadful message from the far-off western sea – a message of war; for it sang a wild, triumphant battle-song, and the strain of the song was:

> I am the mothering White Wind;
> This is my hour of might.
> The hills and the snow are my children;
> My service they do to-night.

And here and there, at the word received, there were mighty doings among the peaks. Here new effects were carven with a stroke; here lakes were made or unmade; here messengers of life and death dispatched. An avalanche from Purcell's Peak went down to gash the sides and show long veins of gold; another hurried, by the White Wind sent, to block a stream and turn its wasted waters to a thirsty land – a messenger of mercy. But down the Gunder Peak there whirled a monstrous mass, charged with a mission of revenge. Down, down, down, loud snoofing as it went, and sliding on from shoulder, ledge, and long incline, now wiping out a forest that would bar its path, then crashing, leaping, rolling, smashing over cliff and steep descent, still gaining as it sped. Down, down, faster, fiercer, in one fell and fearful rush, and Scotty's shanty, in its track, with all that it contained, was crushed and swiftly blotted out. The hunter had forefelt his doom. The Ram's own Mother White Wind, from the western sea, had come – had long delayed, but still had come at last.

These extracts speak for themselves. Seton had style and could convey information clearly, create 'atmosphere' and get any reasonable reader emotionally involved.

One might add that his style does not 'date'. He is as readable now as he was in his lifetime, and for force, control, clarity and economy must be an excellent influence, I would suppose, on any young person trying to learn how to write.

The final thing I would like to stress is this. Seton's 'message' (subordinate, as with all good writers, to the charm and sheer interest of his stories) is not out of date. On the contrary, it is at least as relevant and urgent as ever it was. To-day, the human race is more numerous and powerful than ever before. We can, in effect, control, increase, diminish or destroy any other species we want to. Do we feel as we should for the other species on this planet? Do we identify with them as Seton did? Have we his warmth and sympathy – knowledgeable, realistic and without sentimentality? Are the animals creatures we are entitled to do anything we like to, because we have the power, or are they the creatures towards whom we have a responsibility because we are more powerful and intelligent than they? What would Seton think of the Canadian and Norwegian governments countenancing the battering to death every year, on the Nova Scotia ice, of 150,000 harp seal pups in the presence of their mothers, so that the fur can be used for non-essential trinkets such as the trimming of ski-jackets and key-rings, and the manufacture of paperweights in the form of baby seals? Or the refusal of the Japanese to exercise any responsible control over the slaughter of whales? Or the illegal killing of African elephants for ivory? Of oppressed human minorities in general, whether of Indian or any other race, there is virtually no need to speak. The Cambodian government would not have cared for Mr Seton.

The great C. S. Lewis, in his essay 'On Three Ways of Writing for Children', had this to say:

> The third way, which is the only one I could ever use

myself, consists in writing a children's story because a children's story is the best art-form for something you have to say: just as a composer might write a Dead March not because there was a public funeral in view but because certain musical ideas that had occurred to him went best into that form. This method could apply to other kinds of children's literature besides stories. I have been told that Arthur Mee never met a child and never wished to: it was, from his point of view, a bit of luck that boys liked reading what he liked writing.

For 'Arthur Mee' read 'Ernest Thompson Seton' and one would be spot-on, whether Seton met any children or not. He never wrote down to anyone, young or old. He wrote what he felt, passionately, that he wanted to write. It appealed on merits then. It survives on merits now. That is true art.

Richard Adams

Raggylug

The Story of a Cottontail Rabbit

Raggylug, or Rag, was the name of a young cottontail rabbit. It was given him from his torn and ragged ear, a life-mark that he got in his first adventure. He lived with his mother in Olifant's swamp, where I made their acquaintance and gathered, in a hundred different ways, the little bits of proof and scraps of truth that at length enabled me to write this history.

Those who do not know the animals well may think I have humanized them, but those who have lived so near them as to know somewhat of their ways and their minds will not think so.

Truly rabbits have no speech as we understand it, but they have a way of conveying ideas by a system of sounds, signs, scents, whisker-touches, movements, and example that answers the purpose of speech; and it must be remembered that though in telling this story I freely translate from rabbit into English, *I repeat nothing that they did not say.*

I

The rank swamp grass bent over and concealed the snug nest where Raggylug's mother had hidden him. She had partly covered him with some of the bedding, and, as always, her last warning was to 'lay low and say nothing, whatever happens'. Though tucked in bed, he was wide awake and his bright eyes were taking in that part of his little green world that was straight above. A bluejay and a red-squirrel, two notorious thieves, were loudly berating each other for stealing, and at one time Rag's home bush was the centre of their fight; a yellow warbler caught a blue butterfly but six inches from his nose, and a scarlet and black ladybug, serenely waving her knobbed feelers, took a long walk up one grassblade, down another, and across the nest and over Rag's face – and yet he never moved nor even winked.

After a while he heard a strange rustling of the leaves in the near thicket. It was an odd, continuous sound, and though it went this way and that way and came ever nearer, there was no patter of feet with it. Rag had lived his whole life in the Swamp (he was three weeks old) and yet had never heard anything like this. Of course his curiosity was greatly aroused. His mother had cautioned him to lay low, but that was understood to be in case of danger, and this strange sound without footfalls could not be anything to fear.

The low rasping went past close at hand, then to the right, then back, and seemed going away. Rag felt he knew what he was about; he wasn't a baby; it was his duty to learn what it was. He slowly raised his roly-poly body on his short fluffy legs, lifted his little round head above the covering of his nest and peeped out into the woods. The sound had ceased as soon as he moved. He saw nothing, so took one step forward to a clear view, and instantly found himself face to face with an enormous Black Serpent.

'Mammy,' he screamed in mortal terror as the monster darted at him. With all the strength of his tiny limbs he tried to run. But in a flash the Snake had him by one ear and whipped around him with his coils to gloat over the helpless little baby bunny he had secured for dinner.

'Mam-my – Mam-my,' gasped poor little Raggylug as the cruel monster began slowly choking him to death. Very soon the little one's cry would have ceased, but bounding through the woods straight as an arrow came Mammy. No longer a shy, helpless little Molly Cottontail, ready to fly from a shadow: the mother's love was strong in her. The cry of her baby had filled her with the courage of a hero, and – hop, she went over that horrible reptile. Whack, she struck down at him with her sharp hind claws as she passed, giving him such a stinging blow that he squirmed with pain and hissed with anger.

'M-a-m-m-y,' came feebly from the little one. And Mammy came leaping again and again and struck harder and fiercer until the loathsome reptile let go the little one's ear and tried to bite the old one as she leaped over. But all he got was a mouthful of wool each time, and Molly's fierce blows began to tell, as long bloody rips were torn in the Black Snake's scaly armour.

Things were now looking bad for Snake; and bracing himself for the next charge, he lost his tight hold on Baby Bunny, who at once wriggled out of the coils and away into the underbrush, breathless and terribly frightened, but unhurt save that his left ear was much torn by the teeth of that dreadful Serpent.

Molly now had gained all she wanted. She had no notion of fighting for glory or revenge. Away she went into the woods and the little one followed the shining beacon of her snow-white tail until she led him to a safe corner of the Swamp.

II

Old Olifant's Swamp was a rough, brambly tract of second-growth woods, with a marshy pond and a stream through the middle. A few ragged remnants of the old forest still stood in it and a few of the still older trunks were lying about as dead logs in the brushwood. The land about the pond was of that willow-grown sedgy kind that cats and horses avoid, but that cattle do not fear. The drier zones were overgrown with briers and young trees. The outermost belt of all, that next the fields, was of thrifty, gummy-trunked young pines whose living needles in air and dead ones on earth offer so delicious an odour to the nostrils of the passer-by, and so deadly a breath to those seedlings that would compete with them for the worthless waste they grow on.

All around for a long way were smooth fields, and the only wild tracks that ever crossed these fields were those of a thoroughly bad and unscrupulous fox that lived only too near.

The chief indwellers of the Swamp were Molly and Rag. Their nearest neighbours were far away, and their nearest kin were dead. This was their home, and here they lived together, and here Rag received the training that made his success in life.

Molly was a good little mother and gave him a careful bringing up. The first thing he learned was 'to lay low and say nothing'. His adventure with the snake taught him the wisdom of this. Rag never forgot that lesson; afterwards he did as he was told, and it made the other things come more easily.

The second lesson he learned was 'freeze'. It grows out of the first, and Rag was taught it as soon as he could run.

'Freezing' is simply doing nothing, turning into a statue. As soon as he finds a foe near, no matter what he is doing, a well-trained Cottontail keeps just as he is and stops all movement, for the creatures of the woods are of the same colour as the things in the woods and catch the eye only while moving. So when enemies chance together, the one who first sees the other can keep himself unseen by 'freezing' and thus have all the advantage of choosing the time for attack or escape. Only those who live in the woods know the importance of this; every wild creature and every hunter must learn it; all learn to do it well, but not one of them can beat Molly Cottontail in the doing. Rag's mother taught him this trick by example. When the white cotton cushion that she always carried to sit on went bobbing away through the woods, of course Rag ran his hardest to keep up. But when Molly stopped and 'froze', the natural wish to copy made him do the same.

But the best lesson of all that Rag learned from his mother was the secret of the Brierbrush. It is a very old secret now, and to make it plain you must first hear why the Brierbrush quarrelled with the beasts.

Long ago the Roses used to grow on bushes that had no thorns. But the Squirrels and Mice used to climb after them, the Cattle used to knock them off with their horns, the Possum would twitch them off with his long tail, and the Deer, with his sharp hoofs, would break them down. So the Brierbrush armed itself with spikes to protect its roses and declared eternal war on all creatures that climbed trees, or had horns, or hoofs, or long tails. This left the Brierbrush at peace with none but Molly Cottontail, who could not climb, was hornless, hoofless, and had scarcely any tail at all.

In truth the Cottontail had never harmed a Brierrose, and having now so many enemies the Rose took the Rabbit into especial friendship, and when dangers are threatening poor Bunny he flies to the nearest Brierbrush, certain that it is ready with a million keen and poisoned daggers to defend him.

So the secret that Rag learned from his mother was, 'The Brierbush is your best friend.'

Much of the time that season was spent in learning the lay of the land, and the bramble and brier mazes. And Rag learned them so well that he could go all around the Swamp by two different ways and never leave the friendly briers at any place for more than five hops.

It is not long since the foes of the Cottontails were disgusted to find that man had brought a new kind of bramble and planted it in long lines throughout the country. It was so strong that no creatures could break it down, and so sharp that the toughest skin was torn by it. Each year there was more of it and each year it became a more serious matter to the wild creatures. But Molly Cottontail had no fear of it. She was not brought up in the briers for nothing. Dogs and foxes, cattle and sheep, and even man himself might be torn by those fearful spikes: but Molly understands it and lives and thrives under it. And the further it spreads the more safe country there is for the Cottontail. And the name of this new and dreaded bramble is – *the barbed-wire fence.*

III

Molly had no other children to look after now, so Rag had all her care. He was unusually quick and bright as well as strong, and he had uncommonly good chances; so he got on remarkably well.

All the season she kept him busy learning the tricks of the trail, and what to eat and drink and what not to touch. Day by day she worked to train him; little by little she taught him, putting into his mind hundreds of ideas that her own life or early training had stored in hers, and so equipped him with the knowledge that makes life possible to their kind.

Close by her side in the clover field or the thicket he would sit and copy her when she wobbled her nose 'to keep her smeller clear', and pull the bite from her mouth or taste her lips to make sure he was getting the same kind of fodder. Still copying her, he learned to comb his ears with his claws and to dress his coat and to bite the burrs out of his vest and socks. He learned, too, that nothing but clear dewdrops from the briers were fit for a rabbit to drink, as water which has once touched the earth must surely bear some taint. Thus he began the study of woodcraft, the oldest of all sciences.

As soon as Rag was big enough to go out alone, his mother taught him the signal code. Rabbits telegraph each other by thumping on the ground with their hind feet. Along the ground sound carries far; a thump that at six feet from the earth is not heard at twenty yards will, near the ground, be heard at least one hundred yards. Rabbits have very keen hearing, and so might hear this same thump at two hundred yards, and that would reach from end to end of Olifant's Swamp. A single *thump* means 'look out' or 'freeze'. A slow *thump thump* means 'come'. A fast *thump thump* means 'danger'; and a very fast *thump thump thump* means 'run for dear life'.

At another time, when the weather was fine and the bluejays were quarrelling among themselves, a sure sign that no dangerous foe was about, Rag began a new study. Molly, by flattening her ears, gave the sign to squat. Then she ran far away in the thicket and gave the thumping signal for 'come'. Rag set out at a run to the place but could not find Molly. He thumped, but got no reply. Setting carefully about his search he found her foot-scent and following this strange guide, that the beasts all know so well and man does not know at all, he worked out the trail and found her where she was hidden. Thus he got his first lesson in trailing, and thus it was that the games of hide and seek they played became the schooling for the serious chase of which there was so much in his after life.

Before that first season of schooling was over he had learnt all the principal tricks by which a rabbit lives and in not a few problems showed himself a veritable genius.

He was an adept at 'tree', 'dodge', and 'squat', he could play 'log-lump', with 'wind' and 'baulk' with 'back-track' so well that he scarcely needed any other tricks. He had not yet tried it, but he knew just how to play 'barb-wire', which is a new trick of the brilliant order; he had made a special study of 'sand', which burns up all scent, and he was deeply versed in 'change-off', 'fence', and 'double' as well as 'hole-up', which is a trick requiring longer notice, and yet he never forgot that 'lay-low' is the beginning of all wisdom and 'brierbush' the only trick that is always safe.

He was taught the signs by which to know all his foes and then the way to baffle them. For hawks, owls, foxes, hounds, curs, minks, weasels, cats, skunks, coons, and men, each have a different plan of pursuit, and for each and all of these evils he was taught a remedy.

And for knowledge of the enemy's approach he learned to depend first on himself and his mother, and then on the bluejay. 'Never neglect the bluejay's warning,' said Molly; 'he is a mischief-maker, a marplot, and a thief all the time, but nothing escapes him. He wouldn't mind harming us, but he cannot, thanks to the briers, and his enemies are ours, so it is well to heed him. If the woodpecker cries a warning you can trust him, he is honest; but he is a fool beside the bluejay, and though the bluejay often tells lies for mischief you are safe to believe him when he brings ill news.'

The barb-wire trick takes a deal of nerve and the best of legs. It was long before Rag ventured to play it, but as he came to his full powers it became one of his favourites.

'It's fine play for those who can do it,' said Molly. 'First you lead off your dog on a straightaway and warm him up a bit by nearly letting him catch you. Then keeping just one hop ahead, you lead him at a long slant full tilt into a breast-high barb-wire. I've seen many a dog and fox crippled, and one big hound killed outright this way. But I've also seen more than one rabbit lose his life in trying it.'

Rag early learnt what some rabbits never learn at all, that 'hole-up' is not such a fine ruse as it seems; it may be the certain safety of a wise rabbit, but soon or late is a sure death-trap to a fool. A young rabbit always thinks of it first, an old rabbit never tries it till all others fail. It means escape from a man or dog, a fox or a bird of prey, but it means sudden death if the foe is a ferret, mink, skunk, or weasel.

There were but two ground-holes in the Swamp. One on the Sunning Bank, which was a dry sheltered knoll in the South-end. It was open and sloping to the sun, and here on fine days the Cottontails took their sunbaths. They stretched out among the fragrant pine needles and wintergreen in odd cat-like positions, and turned slowly over as though roasting and wishing all sides well done. And they blinked and panted, and squirmed as if in dreadful pain; yet this was one of the keenest enjoyments they knew.

Just over the brow of the knoll was a large pine stump. Its grotesque roots wriggled out above the yellow sandbank like dragons, and under their protecting claws a sulky old woodchuck had digged a den long ago. He became more sour and ill tempered as weeks went by, and one day waited to quarrel with Olifant's dog instead of going in so that Molly Cottontail was able to take possession of the den an hour later.

This, the pine-root hole, was afterwards very coolly taken by a self-sufficient young skunk who with less valour might have enjoyed greater longevity, for he imagined that even man with a gun would fly from him. Instead of keeping Molly from the den for good, therefore, his reign, like that of a certain Hebrew king, was over in four days.

The other, the fern-hole, was in a fern thicket next the clover field. It was small and damp, and useless except as a last retreat. It also was the work of a woodchuck, a well-meaning friendly neighbour, but a hare-brained youngster whose skin in the form of a whip-lash was now developing higher horse-power in the Olifant working team.

'Simple justice,' said the old man, 'for that hide was raised on stolen feed that the team would a' turned into horse-power anyway.'

The Cottontails were now sole owners of the holes, and did not go near them when they could help it, lest anything like a path should be made that might betray these last retreats to an enemy.

There was also the hollow hickory, which, though nearly fallen, was still green, and had the great advantage of being open at both ends. This had long been the residence of one Lotor, a solitary old coon whose ostensible calling was frog-hunting, and who, like the monks of old, was supposed to abstain from all flesh food. But it was shrewdly suspected that he needed but a chance to indulge in a diet of rabbit. When at last one dark night he was killed while raiding Olifant's hen-house, Molly, so far from feeling a pang of regret, took possession of his cosy nest with a sense of unbounded relief.

IV

Bright August sunlight was flooding the Swamp in the morning. Everything seemed soaking in the warm radiance. A little brown swamp-sparrow was teetering on a long rush in the pond. Beneath him there were open spaces of dirty water that brought down a few scraps of the blue sky, and worked it and the yellow duckweed into an exquisite mosaic, with a little wrong-side picture of the bird in the middle. On the bank behind was a great vigorous growth of golden green skunk-cabbage, that cast dense shadow over the brown swamp tussocks.

The eyes of the swamp-sparrow were not trained to take in the colour glories, but he saw what he might have missed; that two of the numberless leafy brown bumps under the broad cabbage-leaves were furry living things, with noses that never ceased to move up and down whatever else was still.

It was Molly and Rag. They were stretched under the skunk-cabbage, not because they liked its rank smell, but because the winged ticks could not stand it at all and so left them in peace.

Rabbits have no set time for lessons, they are always

learning; but what the lesson is depends on the present stress, and that must arrive before it is known. They went to this place for a quiet rest, but had not been long there when suddenly a warning note from the ever-watchful bluejay caused Molly's nose and ears to go up and her tail to tighten to her back. Away across the Swamp was Olifant's big black and white dog, coming straight towards them.

'Now,' said Molly, 'squat while I go and keep that fool out of mischief.' Away she went to meet him and she fearlessly dashed across the dog's path.

'Bow-ow-ow,' he fairly yelled as he bounded after Molly, but she kept just beyond his reach and led him where the million daggers struck fast and deep, till his tender ears were scratched raw, and guided him at last plump into a hidden barbed-wire fence, where he got such a gashing that he went homeward howling with pain. After making a short double, a loop and a baulk in case the dog should come back, Molly returned to find that Rag in his eagerness was standing bolt upright and craning his neck to see the sport.

This disobedience made her so angry that she struck him with her hind foot and knocked him over in the mud.

One day as they fed on the near clover field a red-tailed hawk came swooping after them. Molly kicked up her hind legs to make fun of him and skipped into the briers along one of their old pathways, where of course the hawk could not follow. It was the main path from the Creekside Thicket to the Stove-pipe brushpile. Several creepers had grown across it, and Molly, keeping one eye on the hawk, set to work and cut the creepers off. Rag watched her, then ran on ahead, and cut some more that were across the path. 'That's right,' said Molly, 'always keep the runways clear, you will need them often enough. Not wide, but clear. Cut everything like a creeper across them and some day you will find you have cut a snare.'

'A what?' asked Rag, as he scratched his right ear with his left hind foot.

'A snare is something that looks like a creeper, but it doesn't grow and it's worse than all the hawks in the world,' said Molly, glancing at the now far-away red-tail, 'for there it hides night and day in the runway till the chance to catch you comes.'

'I don't believe it could catch me,' said Rag, with the pride of youth as he rose on his heels to rub his chin and whiskers high up on a smooth sapling. Rag did not know he was doing this, but his mother saw and knew it was a sign, like the changing of a boy's voice, that her little one was no longer a baby but would soon be a grown-up Cottontail.

V

There is magic in running water. Who does not know it and feel it? The railroad builder fearlessly throws his bank across the wide bog or lake, or the sea itself, but the tiniest rill of running water he treats with great respect, studies its wish and its way and gives it all it seems to ask. The thirst-parched traveller in the poisonous alkali deserts holds back in deadly fear from the sedgy ponds till he finds one down whose centre is a thin, clear line, and a faint flow, the sign of running, living water, and joyfully he drinks.

There is magic in running water, no evil spell can cross it. Tam O'Shanter proved its potency in time of sorest need. The wild-wood creature with its deadly foe following tireless on the trail scent, realizes its nearing doom and feels an awful spell. Its strength is spent, its every trick is tried in vain till the good Angel leads it to the water, the running, living water, and dashing in it follows the cooling stream, and then with force renewed takes to the woods again.

There is magic in running water. The hounds come to the very spot and halt and cast about; and halt and cast in vain. Their spell is broken by the merry stream, and the wild thing lives its life.

And this was one of the great secrets that Raggylug learned from his mother – 'after the Brierrose, the Water is your friend.'

One hot, muggy night in August, Molly led Rag through the woods. The cotton-white cushion she wore under her tail twinkled ahead and was his guiding lantern, though it went out as soon as she stopped and sat on it. After a few runs and stops to listen, they came to the edge of the pond. The hylas in the trees above them were singing '*sleep, sleep*', and away out on a sunken log in the deep water, up to his chin in the cooling bath, a bloated bullfrog was singing the praises of a '*jug o' rum*'.

'Follow me still,' said Molly, in rabbit, and 'flop' she went into the pond and struck out for the sunken log in the middle. Rag flinched but plunged with a little 'ouch', gasping and wobbling his nose very fast but still copying his mother. The same movements as on land sent him through the water, and thus he found he could swim. On he went till he reached the sunken log and scrambled up by his dripping mother on the high dry end, with a rushy screen around them and the Water that tells no tales. After this in warm black nights when that old fox from Springfield came prowling through the Swamp, Rag would note the place of the bullfrog's voice, for in case of direst need it might be a guide to safety. And thenceforth the words of the song that the bullfrog sang were, '*Come, come, in danger come.*'

This was the latest study that Rag took up with his

mother – it was really a post-graduate course, for many little rabbits never learn it at all.

VI

No wild animal dies of old age. Its life has soon or late a tragic end. It is only a question of how long it can hold out against its foes. But Rag's life was proof that once a rabbit passes out of his youth he is likely to outlive his prime and be killed only in the last third of life, the downhill third we call old age.

The Cottontails had enemies on every side. Their daily life was a series of escapes. For dogs, foxes, cats, skunks, coons, weasels, minks, snakes, hawks, owls, and men, and even insects were all plotting to kill them. They had hundreds of adventures, and at least once a day they had to fly for their lives and save themselves by their legs and wits.

More than once that hateful fox from Springfield drove them to taking refuge under the wreck of a barbed-wire hog-pen by the spring. But once there they could look calmly at him while he spiked his legs in vain attempts to reach them.

Once or twice Rag when hunted had played off the hound against a skunk that had seemed likely to be quite as dangerous as the dog.

Once he was caught alive by a hunter who had a hound and a ferret to help him. But Rag had the luck to escape next day, with a yet deeper distrust of ground-holes. He was several times run into the water by the cat, and many times was chased by hawks and owls, but for each kind of danger there was a safeguard. His mother taught him the principal dodges, and he improved on them and made many new ones as he grew older. And the older and wiser he grew the less he trusted to his legs, and the more to his wits for safety.

Ranger was the name of a young hound in the neighbourhood. To train him his master used to put him on the trail of one of the Cottontails. It was nearly always Rag that they ran, for the young buck enjoyed the runs as much as they did, the spice of danger in them being just enough for zest. He would say:

'Oh, mother! here comes the dog again, I must have a run today.'

'You are too bold, Raggy, my son!' she might reply. 'I fear you will run once too often.'

'But mother, it is such glorious fun to tease that fool dog, and it's all good training. I'll thump if I am too hard pressed, then you can come and change off while I get my second wind.'

On he would come, and Ranger would take the trail and follow till Rag got tired of it. Then he either sent a thumping telegram for help, which brought Molly to take charge of the dog, or he got rid of the dog by some clever trick. A description of one of these shows how well Rag had learned the arts of the woods.

He knew that his scent lay best near the ground, and was strongest when he was warm. So if he could get off the

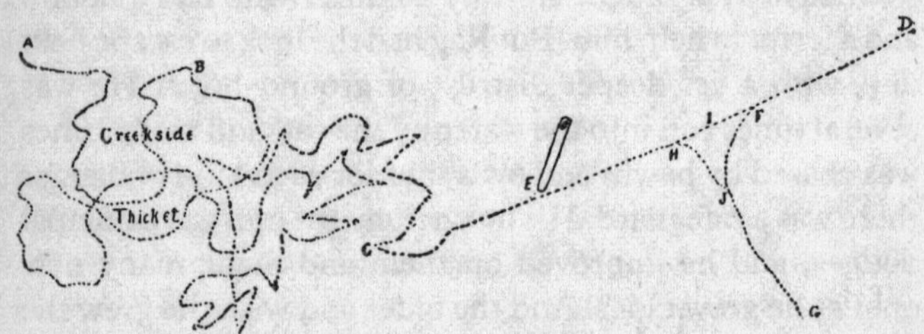

ground, and be left in peace for half an hour to cool off, and for the trail to stale, he knew he would be safe. When, therefore, he tired of the chase, he made for the Creekside brier-patch, where he 'wound' – that is, zigzagged – till he left a course so crooked that the dog was sure to be greatly delayed in working it out. He then went straight to D in the woods, passing one hop to windward of the high log E. Stopping at D, he followed his back trail to F, here he leaped aside and ran towards G. Then, returning on his trail to J, he waited till the hound passed on his trail at I. Rag then got back on his old trail at H, and followed it to E, where, with a scent-baulk or great leap aside, he reached the high log, and running to its higher end, he sat like a bump.

Ranger lost much time in the bramble maze, and the scent was very poor when he got it straightened out, and came to D. Here he began to circle to pick it up, and after losing much time, struck the trail which ended suddenly at G. Again he was at fault, and had to circle to find the trail. Wider and wider the circles, until at last, he passed right under the log Rag was on. But a cold scent, on a cold day, does not go downward much. Rag never budged nor winked, and the hound passed.

Again the dog came round. This time he crossed the low part of the log, and stopped to smell it. 'Yes, clearly it was rabbity,' but it was a stale scent now; still he mounted the log.

It was a trying moment for Rag, as the great hound came sniff-sniffing along the log. But his nerve did not forsake him; the wind was right; he had his mind made up to bolt as soon as Ranger came half way up. But he didn't come. A yellow cur would have seen the rabbit sitting there, but the hound did not, and the scent seemed stale, so he leaped off the log, and Rag had won.

VII

Rag had never seen any other rabbit than his mother. Indeed he had scarcely thought about there being any other. He was more and more away from her now, and yet he never felt lonely, for rabbits do not hanker for company. But one day in December, while he was among the red dogwood brush, cutting a new path to the great Creekside thicket, he saw all at once against the sky over the Sunning Bank the head and ears of a strange rabbit. The new-comer had the air of a well-pleased discoverer and soon came hopping Rag's way along one of *his* paths into *his* Swamp. A new feeling rushed over him, that boiling mixture of anger and hatred called jealousy.

The stranger stopped at one of Rag's rubbing-trees – that is, a tree against which he used to stand on his heels and rub his chin as far up as he could reach. He thought he did this simply because he liked it; but all buck-rabbits do so, and several ends are served. It makes the tree rabbity, so that other rabbits know that this swamp already belongs to a rabbit family and is not open for settlement. It also lets the next one know by the scent if the last caller was an acquaintance, and the height from the ground of the rubbing-places shows how tall the rabbit is.

Now to his disgust Rag noticed that the new-comer was a head taller than himself, and a big, stout buck at that. This was a wholly new experience and filled Rag with a wholly new feeling. The spirit of murder entered his heart; he chewed very hard with nothing in his mouth, and hopping forward on to a smooth piece of hard ground he struck slowly:

'*Thump – thump – thump*,' which is a rabbit telegram for, 'Get out of my swamp, or fight.'

The new-comer made a big V with his ears, sat upright for a few seconds, then, dropping on his fore-feet, sent along the ground a louder, stronger, '*Thump – thump – thump*.'

And so war was declared.

They came together by short runs side-wise, each one trying to get the wind of the other and watching for a chance advantage. The stranger was a big, heavy buck with plenty of muscle, but one or two trifles such as treading on a turnover and failing to close when Rag was on low ground showed that he had not much cunning and counted on winning his battles by his weight. On he came at last and Rag met him like a little fury. As they came together they leaped up and struck out with their hind feet. *Thud*, *thud* they came, and down went poor little Rag. In a moment the stranger was on him with his teeth and Rag was bitten, and lost several tufts of hair before he could get up. But he was swift of foot and got out of reach. Again he charged and again he was knocked down and bitten severely. He was no match for his foe, and it soon became a question of saving his own life.

Hurt as he was he sprang away, with the stranger in full chase, and bound to kill him as well as to oust him from the Swamp where he was born. Rag's legs were good and so was his wind. The stranger was big and so heavy that he soon gave up the chase, and it was well for poor Rag that he did, for he was getting stiff from his wounds as well as tired. From that day began a reign of terror for Rag. His training had been against owls, dogs, weasels, men, and so on, but what to do when chased by another rabbit, he did not know. All he knew was to lay low till he was found, then run.

Poor little Molly was completely terrorized; she could not help Rag and sought only to hide. But the big buck soon found her out. She tried to run from him, but she was not now so swift as Rag. The stranger made no attempt to kill her, but he made love to her, and because she hated him and tried to get away, he treated her shamefully. Day after day he worried her by following her about, and often, furious at her lasting hatred, he would knock her down and tear out mouthfuls of her soft fur till his rage cooled somewhat, when he would let her go for a while. But his fixed purpose was to kill Rag, whose escape seemed hopeless. There was no other swamp he could go to, and whenever he took a nap now he had to be ready at any moment to dash for his life. A dozen times a day the big stranger came creeping up to where he slept, but each time the watchful Rag awoke in time to escape. To escape yet not to escape. He saved his life indeed, but oh! what a miserable life it had become. How maddening to be thus helpless, to see his little mother daily beaten and torn, as well as to see all his favourite feeding-grounds, the cosy nooks, and the pathways he had made with so much labour, forced from him by this hateful brute. Unhappy Rag realized that to the victor belong the spoils, and he hated him more than ever he did a fox or ferret.

How was it to end? He was wearing out with running and watching and bad food, and little Molly's strength and spirit were breaking down under the long persecution. The stranger was ready to go to all lengths to destroy poor Rag, and at last stooped to the worst crime known among rabbits. However much they may hate each other, all good rabbits forget their feuds when their common enemy appears. Yet one day when a great goshawk came swooping over the Swamp, the stranger, keeping well under cover himself, tried again and again to drive Rag into the open.

Once or twice the hawk nearly had him, but still the briers saved him, and it was only when the big buck himself came near being caught that he gave it up. And again Rag escaped, but was no better off. He made up his mind to leave, with his mother, if possible, next night and go into the world in quest of some new home when he heard old Thunder, the hound, sniffing and searching about the outskirts of the Swamp, and he resolved on playing a desperate game. He deliberately crossed the hound's view, and the chase that then began was fast and furious. Thrice around the Swamp they went till Rag had made sure that his mother was hidden safely and that his hated foe was in his usual nest. Then right into that nest and plump over him he jumped, giving him a rap with one hind foot as he passed over his head.

'You miserable fool, I kill you yet,' cried the stranger, and up he jumped only to find himself between Rag and the dog and heir to all the peril of the chase.

On came the hound baying hotly on the straight-away scent. The buck's weight and size were great advantages in a rabbit fight, but now they were fatal. He did not know many tricks. Just the simple ones like 'double', 'wind', and 'hole-up', that every baby Bunny knows. But the chase was too close for doubling and winding, and he didn't know where the holes were.

It was a straight race. The brierrose, kind to all rabbits alike, did its best, but it was no use. The baying of the hound was fast and steady. The crashing of the brush and the yelping of the hound each time the briers tore his tender ears were borne to the two rabbits where they crouched in hiding. But suddenly these sounds stopped, there was a scuffle, then loud and terrible screaming.

Rag knew what it meant and it sent a shiver through him, but he soon forgot that when all was over and rejoiced to be once more the master of the dear old Swamp.

VIII

Old Olifant had doubtless a right to burn all those brush-piles in the east and south of the Swamp and to clear up the wreck of the old barbed-wire hog-pen just below the spring. But it was none the less hard on Rag and his mother. The first were their various residences and outposts, and the second their grand fastness and safe retreat.

They had so long held the Swamp and felt it to be their very own in every part and suburb – including Olifant's grounds and buildings – that they would have resented the appearance of another rabbit even about the adjoining barnyard.

Their claim, that of long, successful occupancy, was exactly the same as that by which most nations hold their land, and it would be hard to find a better right.

During the time of the January thaw the Olifants had cut the rest of the large wood about the pond and curtailed the Cottontails' domain on all sides. But they still clung to the dwindling Swamp, for it was their home and they were loath to move to foreign parts. Their life of daily perils went on, but they were still fleet of foot, long of wind, and bright of wit. Of late they had been somewhat troubled by a mink that had wandered up-stream to their quiet nook. A little judicious guidance had transferred the uncomfortable visitor to Olifant's hen-house. But they were not yet quite sure that he had been properly looked after. So for the present they gave up using the ground-holes, which were, of course, dangerous blind-alleys, and stuck closer than ever to the briers and the brush-piles that were left.

That first snow had quite gone and the weather was bright and warm until now. Molly, feeling a touch of rheumatism, was somewhere in the lower thicket seeking a teaberry tonic. Rag was sitting in the weak sunlight on a bank in the east side. The smoke from the familiar gable chimney of Olifant's house came fitfully drifting a pale blue haze through the underwoods and showing as a dull brown against the brightness of the sky. The sun-gilt gable was cut off midway by the banks of brierbrush, that purple in shadow shone like rods of blazing crimson and gold in the light. Beyond the house the barn with its gable and roof, new gilt as the house, stood up like a Noah's ark.

The sounds that came from it, and yet more the delicious smell that mingled with the smoke, told Rag that the animals were being fed cabbage in the yard. Rag's mouth watered at the idea of the feast. He blinked and blinked as he snuffed its odorous promises, for he loved cabbage dearly. But then he had been to the barnyard the night before after a few paltry clover-tops, and no wise rabbit would go two nights running to the same place.

Therefore he did the wise thing. He moved across where he could not smell the cabbage and made his supper of a bundle of hay that had been blown from the stack. Later, when about to settle for the night, he was joined by Molly, who had taken her teaberry and then eaten her frugal meal of sweet birch near the Sunning Bank.

Meanwhile the sun had gone about his business elsewhere, taking all his gold and glory with him. Off in the east a big black shutter came pushing up and rising higher and higher; it spread over the whole sky, shut out all light and left the world a very gloomy place indeed. Then another mischief-maker, the wind, taking advantage of the sun's absence, came on the scene and set about brewing trouble. The weather turned colder and colder; it seemed worse than when the ground had been covered with snow.

'Isn't this terribly cold? How I wish we had our stove-pipe brush-pile,' said Rag.

'A good night for the pine-root hole,' replied Molly, 'but we have not yet seen the pelt of that mink on the end of the barn, and it is not safe till we do.'

The hollow hickory was gone – in fact at this very moment its trunk, lying in the wood-yard, was harbouring the mink they feared. So the Cottontails hopped to the south side of the pond and, choosing a brush-pile, they crept under and snuggled down for the night, facing the wind but with their noses in different directions so as to go out different ways in case of alarm. The wind blew harder and colder as the hours went by, and about midnight a fine icy snow came ticking down on the dead leaves and hissing through a brush heap. It might seem a poor night for hunting, but that old fox from Springfield was out. He came pointing up the wind in the shelter of the Swamp and chanced in the lee of the brush-pile, where he scented the sleeping Cottontails. He halted for a moment, then came stealthily sneaking up towards the brush under which his nose told him the rabbits were crouching. The noise of the wind and the sleet enabled him to come quite close before Molly heard the faint crunch of a dry leaf under his paw. She touched Rag's whiskers, and both were fully awake just as the fox sprang on them; but they always slept with their legs ready for a jump. Molly darted out into the blinding storm. The fox missed his spring but followed like a racer, while Rag dashed off to one side.

There was only one road for Molly; that was straight up the wind, and bounding for her life she gained a little over the unfrozen mud that would not carry the fox, till she reached the margin of the pond. No chance to turn now, on she must go.

Splash! splash! through the weeds she went, then plunge into the deep water.

And plunge went the fox close behind. But it was too

much for Reynard on such a night. He turned back, and Molly, seeing only one course, struggled through the reeds into the deep water and struck out for the other shore. But there was a strong headwind. The little waves, icy cold, broke over her head as she swam, and the water was full of snow that blocked her way like soft ice, or floating mud. The dark line of the other shore seemed far, far away, with perhaps the fox waiting for her there.

But she laid her ears flat to be out of the gale, and bravely put forth all her strength with wind and tide against her. After a long, weary swim in the cold water, she had nearly reached the farther reeds when a great mass of floating snow barred her road; then the wind on the bank made strange, fox-like sounds that robbed her of all force, and she was drifted far backward before she could get free from the floating bar.

Again she struck out, but slowly – oh so slowly now. And when at last she reached the lee of the tall reeds, her limbs were numbed, her strength spent, her brave little heart was sinking, and she cared no more whether the fox were there or not. Through the reeds she did indeed pass, but once in the weeds her course wavered and slowed, her feeble strokes no longer sent her landward, the ice forming around her, stopped her altogether. In a little while the cold, weak limbs ceased to move, the furry nosetip of the little mother Cottontail wobbled no more, and the soft brown eyes were closed in death.

But there was no fox waiting to tear her with ravenous jaws. Rag had escaped the first onset of the foe, and as soon as he regained his wits he came running back to change-off and so help his mother. He met the old fox going round the pond to meet Molly and led him far and away, then dismissed him with a barbed-wire gash on his head, and came to the bank and sought about and trailed and thumped, but all his searching was in vain; he could not find his little mother. He never saw her again, and he never knew whither she went, for she slept her never-waking sleep in the ice arms of her friend the Water that tells no tales.

Poor little Molly Cottontail! She was a true heroine, yet only one of unnumbered millions that without a thought of heroism have lived and done their best in their little world, and died. She fought a good fight in the battle of life. She was good stuff; the stuff that never dies. For flesh of her flesh and brain of her brain was Rag. She lives in him, and through him transmits a finer fibre to her race.

And Rag still lives in the Swamp. Old Olifant died that winter, and the unthrifty sons ceased to clear the Swamp or mend the wire fences. Within a single year it was a wilder place than ever; fresh trees and brambles grew, and falling wires made many Cottontail castles and last retreats that dogs and foxes dared not storm. And there to this day lives Rag. He is a big strong buck now and fears no rivals. He has a large family of his own, and a pretty brown wife that he got I know not where. There, no doubt, he and his children's children will flourish for many years to come, and there you may see them any sunny evening if you have learnt their signal code, and choosing a good spot on the ground, know just how and when to thump it.

Lobo

The King of Currumpaw

I

Currumpaw is a vast cattle range in northern New Mexico. It is a land of rich pastures and teeming flocks and herds, a land of rolling mesas and precious running waters that at length unite in the Currumpaw River, from which the whole region is named. And the king whose despotic power was felt over its entire extent was an old grey wolf.

Old Lobo, or the king, as the Mexicans called him, was the gigantic leader of a remarkable pack of grey wolves, that had ravaged the Currumpaw Valley for a number of years. All the shepherds and ranchmen knew him well, and, wherever he appeared with his trusty band, terror reigned supreme among the cattle, and wrath and despair among their owners. Old Lobo was a giant among wolves, and was cunning and strong in proportion to his size. His voice at night was well-known and easily distinguished from that of any of his fellows. An ordinary wolf might howl half the night about the herdsman's bivouac without attracting more than a passing notice, but when the deep roar of the old king came booming down the cañon, the watcher bestirred himself and prepared to learn in the morning that fresh and serious inroads had been made among the herds.

Old Lobo's band was but a small one. This I never quite understood, for usually, when a wolf rises to the position and power that he had, he attracts a numerous following. It may be that he had as many as he desired, or perhaps his ferocious temper prevented the increase of his pack. Certain is it that Lobo had only five followers during the latter part of his reign. Each of these, however, was a wolf of renown, most of them were above the ordinary size, one in particular, the second in command, was a veritable giant, but even he was far below the leader in size and prowess. Several of the band, besides the two leaders, were especially noted. One of those was a beautiful white wolf, that the Mexicans called Blanca; this was supposed to be a female, possibly Lobo's mate. Another was a yellow wolf of remarkable swiftness, which, according to current stories had, on several occasions, captured an antelope for the pack.

It will be seen, then, that these wolves were thoroughly well-known to the cowboys and shepherds. They were frequently seen and oftener heard, and their lives were intimately associated with those of the cattlemen, who would so gladly have destroyed them. There was not a stockman on the Currumpaw who would not readily have given the value of many steers for the scalp of any one of Lobo's band, but they seemed to possess charmed lives, and defied all manner of devices to kill them. They scorned all hunters, derided all poisons, and continued, for at least five years, to exact their tribute from the Currumpaw ranchers to the extent, many said, of a cow each day. According to this estimate, therefore, the band had killed more than two thousand of the finest stock, for, as was only too well-known, they selected the best in every instance.

The old idea that a wolf was constantly in a starving state, and therefore ready to eat anything, was as far as possible from the truth in this case, for these freebooters were always sleek and well-conditioned, and were in fact most fastidious about what they ate. Any animal that had died from natural causes, or that was diseased or tainted, they would not touch, and they even rejected anything that had been killed by the stockmen. Their choice and daily food was the tenderer part of a freshly killed yearling heifer. An old bull or cow they disdained, and though they occasionally took a young calf or colt, it was quite clear that veal or horseflesh was not their favourite diet. It was also known that they were not fond of mutton, although they often amused themselves by killing sheep. One night in November, 1893, Blanca and the yellow wolf killed two hundred and fifty sheep, apparently for the fun of it, and did not eat an ounce of their flesh.

These are examples of many stories which I might repeat, to show the ravages of this destructive band. Many new devices for their extinction were tried each year, but still they lived and throve in spite of all the efforts of their foes. A great price was set on Lobo's head, and in consequence poison in a score of subtle forms was put out for him, but he never failed to detect and avoid it. One thing only he feared – that was firearms, and knowing full well that all men in this region carried them, he never was known to attack or face a human being. Indeed, the set policy of his band was to take refuge in flight whenever, in the daytime, a man was descried, no matter at what distance. Lobo's habit of permitting the pack to eat only that which they themselves had killed, was in numerous cases their salvation, and the keenness of his scent to detect the taint of human hands or the poison itself, completed their immunity.

On one occasion, one of the cowboys heard the too familiar rallying-cry of Old Lobo, and stealthily approaching, he found the Currumpaw pack in a hollow, where they had 'rounded up' a small herd of cattle. Lobo sat apart on a knoll, while Blanca with the rest was endeavouring to 'cut out' a young cow, which they had selected; but the cattle were standing in a compact mass with their heads outward, and presented to the foe a line of horns, unbroken save when some cow, frightened by a fresh onset of the wolves, tried to retreat into the middle of the herd. It was only by taking advantage of these breaks that the wolves had succeeded at all in wounding the selected cow, but she was far from being disabled, and it seemed that Lobo at length lost patience with his followers, for he left his position on the hill, and, uttering a deep roar, dashed towards the herd. The terrified rank broke at his charge, and he sprang in among them. Then the cattle scattered like the pieces of a bursting bomb. Away went the chosen victim, but ere she had gone twenty-five yards Lobo was upon her. Seizing her by the neck he suddenly held back with all his force and so threw her heavily to the ground. The shock must have been tremendous, for the heifer was thrown heels over head. Lobo also turned a somersault, but immediately recovered himself, and his followers falling on the poor cow, killed her in a few seconds. Lobo took no part in the killing – after having thrown the victim, he seemed to say, 'Now, why could not some of you have done that at once without wasting so much time?'

The man now rode up shouting, the wolves as usual retired, and he, having a bottle of strychnine, quickly poisoned the carcass in three places, then went away, knowing they would return to feed, as they had killed the animal themselves. But next morning, on going to look for his expected victims, he found that, although the wolves had eaten the heifer, they had carefully cut out and thrown aside all those parts that had been poisoned.

The dread of this great wolf spread yearly among the ranchmen, and each year a larger price was set on his head, until at last it reached $1,000, an unparalleled wolf-bounty, surely; many a good man has been hunted down for less. Tempted by the promised reward, a Texan ranger named Tannerey came one day galloping up the cañon of the Currumpaw. He had a superb outfit for wolf-hunting – the best of guns and horses, and a pack of enormous wolf-hounds. Far out on the plains of the Pan-handle, he and his dogs had killed many a wolf, and now he never doubted that, within a few days, Old Lobo's scalp would dangle at his saddle-bow.

Away they went bravely on their hunt in the grey dawn of a summer morning, and soon the great dogs gave joyous tongue to say that they were already on the track of their quarry. Within two miles, the grizzly band of Currumpaw leaped into view, and the chase grew fast and furious. The part of the wolf-hounds was merely to hold the wolves at bay till the hunter could ride up and shoot them, and this usually was easy on the open plains of Texas; but here a new feature of the country came into play, and showed how well Lobo had chosen his range; for the rocky cañons of the Currumpaw and its tributaries intersect the prairies in every direction. The old wolf at once made for the nearest of these and by crossing it got rid of the horsemen. His band then scattered and thereby scattered the dogs, and when they reunited at a distant point of course all of the dogs did not turn up, and the wolves no longer outnumbered, turned on their pursuers and killed or desperately wounded them all. That night when Tannerey mustered his dogs, only six of them returned, and of these, two were terribly lacerated. This hunter made two other attempts to capture the royal scalp, but neither of them was more successful than the first, and on the last occasion his best horse met its death by a fall; so he gave up the chase in disgust and went back to Texas, leaving Lobo more than ever the despot of the region.

Next year, two other hunters appeared, determined to win the promised bounty. Each believed he could destroy this noted wolf, the first by means of a newly devised poison, which was to be laid out in an entirely new manner; the other a French Canadian, by poison assisted with certain spells and charms, for he firmly believed that Lobo was a veritable 'loup-garou', and could not be killed by ordinary means. But cunningly compounded poisons, charms, and incantations were all of no avail against this grizzly devastator. He made his weekly rounds and daily banquets as aforetime, and before many weeks had passed, Calone and Laloche gave up in despair and went elsewhere to hunt.

In the spring of 1893, after his unsuccessful attempt to capture Lobo, Joe Calone had a humiliating experience, which seems to show that the big wolf simply scorned his enemies, and had absolute confidence in himself. Calone's farm was on a small tributary of the Currumpaw, in a picturesque cañon, and among the rocks of this very cañon, within a thousand yards of the house, Old Lobo and his mate selected their den and raised their family that season. There they lived all summer, and killed Joe's cattle, sheep, and dogs, but laughed at all his poisons and traps, and rested securely among the recesses of the cavernous cliffs, while Joe vainly racked his brain for some method of smoking them out, or of reaching them with dynamite. But they escaped entirely unscathed, and continued their ravages as before. 'There's where he lived all last summer,' said Joe, pointing to the face of the cliff, 'and I couldn't do a thing with him. I was like a fool to him.'

II

This history, gathered so far from the cowboys, I found hard to believe until in the fall of 1893, I made the acquaintance of the wily marauder, and at length came to know him more thoroughly than anyone else. Some years before, in the Bingo days, I had been a wolf-hunter, but my occupations since then had been of another sort, chaining me to stool and desk. I was much in need of a change, and when a friend, who was also a ranch-owner on the Currumpaw, asked me to come to New Mexico and try if I could do anything with this predatory pack, I accepted the invitation and, eager to make the acquaintance of its king, was as soon as possible among the mesas of that region. I spent some time riding about to learn the country, and at intervals, my guide would point to the skeleton of a cow to which the hide still adhered, and remark, 'That's some of his work.'

It became quite clear to me that, in this rough country, it was useless to think of pursuing Lobo with hounds and horses, so that poison or traps were the only available expedients. At present we had no traps large enough, so I set to work with poison.

I need not enter into the details of a hundred devices that I employed to circumvent this 'loup-garou'; there was no combination of strychnine, arsenic, cyanide, or prussic acid, that I did not essay; there was no manner of flesh that I did not try as bait; but morning after morning, as I rode forth to learn the result, I found that all my efforts had been useless. The old king was too cunning for me. A single instance will show his wonderful sagacity. Acting on the hint of an old trapper, I melted some cheese together with the kidney fat of a freshly killed heifer, stewing it in a china dish, and cutting it with a bone knife to avoid the taint of metal. When the mixture was cool, I cut it into lumps, and making a hole in one side of each lump, I inserted a large dose of strychnine and cyanide, contained in a capsule that was impermeable by any odour; finally I sealed the holes up with pieces of the cheese itself. During the whole process, I wore a pair of gloves steeped in the hot blood of the heifer, and even avoided breathing on the baits. When all was ready, I put them in a raw-hide bag rubbed all over with blood, and rode forth dragging the liver and kidneys of the beef at the end of a rope. With this I made a ten-mile circuit, dropping a bait at each quarter of a mile, and taking the utmost care, always, not to touch any with my hands.

Lobo, generally, came into this part of the range in the early part of each week, and passed the latter part, it was supposed, around the base of Sierra Grande. This was Monday, and that same evening, as we were about to retire, I heard the deep bass howl of his majesty. On hearing it one of the boys briefly remarked, 'There he is, we'll see.'

The next morning I went forth, eager to know the result. I soon came on the fresh trail of the robbers, with Lobo in the lead – his track was always easily distinguished. An ordinary wolf's forefoot is $4\frac{1}{2}$ inches long, that of a large wolf $4\frac{3}{4}$ inches, but Lobo's, as measured a number of times, was $5\frac{1}{2}$ inches from claw to heel; I afterwards found that his other proportions were commensurate, for he stood three feet high at the shoulder, and weighed 150 pounds. His trail, therefore, though obscured by those of his followers, was never difficult to trace. The pack had soon found the track of my drag, and as usual followed it. I could see that Lobo had come to the first bait, sniffed about it, and finally had picked it up.

Then I could not conceal my delight. 'I've got him at last,' I exclaimed; 'I shall find him stark within a mile,' and

I galloped on with eager eyes fixed on the great broad track in the dust. It led me to the second bait and that also was gone. How I exulted – I surely have him now and perhaps several of his band. But there was the broad paw-mark still on the drag; and though I stood in the stirrup and scanned the plain I saw nothing that looked like a dead wolf. Again I followed – to find now that the third bait was gone – and the king-wolf's track led on to the fourth, there to learn that he had not really taken a bait at all, but had merely carried them in his mouth. Then having piled the three on the fourth, he scattered filth over them to express his utter contempt for my devices. After this he left my drag and went about his business with the pack he guarded so effectively.

This is only one of many similar experiences which convinced me that poison would never avail to destroy this robber, and though I continued to use it while awaiting the arrival of the traps, it was only because it was meanwhile a sure means of killing many prairie wolves and other destructive vermin.

About this time there came under my observation an incident that will illustrate Lobo's diabolic cunning. These wolves had at least one pursuit which was merely an amusement, it was stampeding and killing sheep, though they rarely ate them. The sheep are usually kept in flocks of from one thousand to three thousand under one or more shepherds. At night they are gathered in the most sheltered place available, and a herdsman sleeps on each side of the flock to give additional protection. Sheep are such senseless creatures that they are liable to be stampeded by the veriest trifle, but they have deeply ingrained in their nature one, and perhaps only one, strong weakness, namely, to follow their leader. And this the shepherds turn to good account by putting half a dozen goats in the flock of sheep. The latter recognize the superior intelligence of their bearded cousins, and when a night alarm occurs they crowd around them, and usually are thus saved from a stampede and are easily protected. But it was not always so. One night late in the last November, two Perico shepherds were aroused by an onset of wolves. Their flocks huddled around the goats, which being neither fools nor cowards, stood their ground and were bravely defiant; but alas for them, no common wolf was heading this attack. Old Lobo, the werewolf, knew as well as the shepherds that the goats were the moral force of the flock, so hastily running over the backs of the densely packed sheep, he fell on these leaders, slew them all in a few minutes, and soon had the luckless sheep stampeding in a thousand different directions. For weeks afterwards I was almost daily accosted by some anxious shepherd, who asked, 'Have you seen any stray OTO sheep lately?' and usually I was obliged to say I had; one day it was, 'Yes, I came on some five or six carcasses by Diamond Springs'; or another, it was to the effect that I had seen a small 'bunch' running on the Malpai Mesa; or again, 'No, but Juan Meira saw about twenty, freshly killed, on the Cedra Monte two days ago.'

At length the wolf-traps arrived, and with two men I worked a whole week to get them properly set out. We spared no labour or pains, I adopted every device I could think of that might help to insure success. The second day after the traps arrived, I rode around to inspect, and soon came upon Lobo's trail running from trap to trap. In the dust I could read the whole story of his doings that night. He had trotted along in the darkness, and although the traps were so carefully concealed, he had instantly detected the first one. Stopping the onward march of the pack, he had cautiously scratched around it until he had disclosed the trap, the chain, and the log, then left them wholly exposed to view with the trap still unsprung, and passing on he treated over a dozen traps in the same fashion. Very soon I noticed that he stopped and turned aside as soon as he detected suspicious signs on the trail and a new plan to outwit him at once suggested itself. I set the traps in the form of an H; that is, with a row of traps on each side of the trail, and one on the trail for the cross-bar of the H. Before long, I had an opportunity to count another failure. Lobo came trotting along the trail, and was fairly between the parallel lines before he detected the single trap in the trail, but he stopped in time, and why or how he knew enough I cannot tell, the Angel of the wild things must have been with him, but without turning an inch to the right or left, he slowly and cautiously backed on his own tracks, putting each paw exactly in its old track until he was off the dangerous ground. Then returning at one side he scratched clods and stones with his hind feet till he had sprung every trap. This he did on many other occasions, and although I varied my methods and redoubled my precautions, he was never deceived, his sagacity seemed never at fault, and he might have been pursuing his career of rapine today, but for an unfortunate alliance that proved his ruin and added his name to the long list of heroes who, unassailable when alone, have fallen through the indiscretion of a trusted ally.

III

Once or twice, I had found indications that everything was not quite right in the Currumpaw pack. There were signs of irregularity, I thought; for instance there was clearly the trail of a smaller wolf running ahead of the leader, at times, and this I could not understand until a cowboy made a remark which explained the matter.

'I saw them today,' he said, 'and the wild one that breaks away is Blanca.' Then the truth dawned upon me, and I added, 'Now, I know that Blanca is a she-wolf, because were a he-wolf to act thus, Lobo would kill him at once.'

This suggested a new plan. I killed a heifer, and set one or two rather obvious traps about the carcass. Then cutting off the head, which is considered useless offal, and quite beneath the notice of a wolf, I set it a little apart and around it placed six powerful steel traps properly deodorized and concealed with the utmost care. During my operations I kept my hands, boots, and implements smeared with fresh blood, and afterwards sprinkled the ground with the same, as though it had flowed from the head; and when the traps were buried in the dust I brushed the place over with the skin of a coyote, and with a foot of the same animal made a number of tracks over the traps. The head was so placed that there was a narrow passage between it and some tussocks, and in this passage I buried two of my best traps, fastening them to the head itself.

Wolves have a habit of approaching every carcass they get the wind of, in order to examine it, even when they have no intention of eating of it, and I hoped that this habit would bring the Currumpaw pack within reach of my latest stratagem. I did not doubt that Lobo would detect my handiwork about the meat, and prevent the pack approaching it, but I did build some hopes on the head, for it looked as though it had been thrown aside as useless.

Next morning, I sallied forth to inspect the traps, and there, oh, joy! were the tracks of the pack, and the place where the beef-head and its traps had been was empty. A hasty study of the trail showed that Lobo had kept the pack from approaching the meat, but one, a small wolf, had evidently gone on to examine the head as it lay apart and had walked right into one of the traps.

We set out on the trail, and within a mile discovered that the hapless wolf was Blanca. Away she went, however, at a gallop, and although encumbered by the beef-head, which weighed over fifty pounds, she speedily distanced my companion who was on foot. But we overtook her when she reached the rocks, for the horns of the cow's head became caught and held her fast. She was the handsomest wolf I had ever seen. Her coat was in perfect condition and nearly white.

She turned to fight, and raising her voice in the rallying cry of her race, sent a long howl rolling over the cañon. From far away upon the mesa came a deep response, the cry of Old Lobo. That was her last call, for now we had closed in on her, and all her energy and breath were devoted to combat.

Then followed the inevitable tragedy, the idea of which I shrank from afterwards more than at the time. We each threw a lasso over the neck of the doomed wolf, and strained our horses in opposite directions until the blood burst from her mouth, her eyes glazed, her limbs stiffened and then fell limp. Homeward then we rode, carrying the dead wolf, and exulting over this, the first death-blow we had been able to inflict on the Currumpaw pack.

At intervals during the tragedy, and afterwards as we rode homeward, we heard the roar of Lobo as he wandered about on the distant mesas, where he seemed to be searching for Blanca. He had never really deserted her, but knowing that he could not save her, his deep-rooted dread of firearms had been too much for him when he saw us approaching. All that day we heard him wailing as he roamed in his quest, and I remarked at length to one of the boys, 'Now, indeed, I truly know that Blanca was his mate.'

As evening fell he seemed to be coming towards the home cañon, for his voice sounded continually nearer. There was an unmistakable note of sorrow in it now. It was no longer the loud, defiant howl, but a long, plaintive wail; 'Blanca! Blanca!' he seemed to call. And as night came down, I noticed that he was not far from the place where we had overtaken her. At length he seemed to find the trail, and when he came to the spot where we had killed her, his heart-broken wailing was piteous to hear. It was sadder than I could possibly have believed. Even the stolid cowboys noticed it, and said they had 'never heard a wolf carry on like that before'. He seemed to know exactly what had taken place, for her blood had stained the place of her death.

Then he took up the trail of the horses and followed it to the ranch-house. Whether in hopes of finding her there, or in quest of revenge, I know not, but the latter was what he found, for he surprised our unfortunate watchdog outside and tore him to little bits within fifty yards of the door. He evidently came alone this time, for I found but one trail next morning, and he had galloped about in a reckless manner that was very unusual with him. I had half expected this, and had set a number of additional traps about the pasture. Afterwards I found that he had indeed fallen into one of these, but such was his strength, he had torn himself loose and cast it aside.

I believed that he would continue in the neighbourhood until he found her body at least, so I concentrated all my energies on this one enterprise of catching him before he left the region, and while yet in this reckless mood. Then I realized what a mistake I had made in killing Blanca, for by using her as a decoy I might have secured him the next night.

I gathered in all the traps I could command, one hundred and thirty strong steel wolf-traps, and set them in fours in every trail that led into the cañon; each trap was separately fastened to a log, and each log was separately buried. In burying them, I carefully removed the sod and every particle of earth that was lifted we put in blankets, so that after the sod was replaced and all was finished the eye could detect no trace of human handiwork. When the traps were concealed I trailed the body of poor Blanca over each place, and made of it a drag that circled all about the ranch, and finally I took off one of her paws and made with it a line of tracks over each trap. Every precaution and device known to me I used, and retired at a late hour to await the result.

Once during the night I thought I heard Old Lobo, but was not sure of it. Next day I rode around, but darkness came on before I completed the circuit of the north cañon, and I had nothing to report. At supper one of the cowboys said, 'There was a great row among the cattle in the north cañon this morning, maybe there is something in the traps there.' It was afternoon of the next day before I got to the place referred to, and as I drew near a great grizzly form arose from the ground, vainly endeavouring to escape, and there revealed before me stood Lobo, King of the Currumpaw, firmly held in the traps. Poor old hero, he had never ceased to search for his darling, and when he found the trail her body had made he followed it recklessly, and so fell into the snare prepared for him. There he lay in the iron grasp of all four traps, perfectly helpless, and all around him were numerous tracks showing how the cattle had gathered about him to insult the fallen despot, without daring to approach within his reach. For two days and two nights he had lain there, and now was worn out with struggling. Yet, when I went near him, he rose up with bristling mane and raised his voice, and for the last time made the cañon reverberate with his deep bass roar, a call for help, the muster call of his band. But there was none to answer him, and, left alone in his extremity, he whirled about with all his strength and made a desperate effort to get at me. All in vain, each trap was a dead drag of over three hundred pounds, and in their relentless fourfold grasp, with great steel jaws on every foot, and the heavy logs and chains all entangled together, he was absolutely powerless. How his huge ivory tusks did grind on those cruel chains, and when I ventured to touch him with my rifle-barrel he left grooves on it which are there to this day. His eyes glared green with hate and fury, and his jaws snapped with a hollow 'chop', as he vainly endeavoured to reach me and my trembling horse. But he was worn out with hunger and struggling and loss of blood, and he soon sank exhausted to the ground.

Something like compunction came over me, as I prepared to deal out to him that which so many had suffered at his hands.

'Grand old outlaw, hero of a thousand lawless raids, in a few minutes you will be but a great load of carrion. It cannot be otherwise.' Then I swung my lasso and sent it whistling over his head. But not so fast; he was yet far from being subdued, and, before the supple coils had fallen on his neck he seized the noose and, with one fierce chop, cut through its hard thick strands, and dropped it in two pieces at his feet.

Of course I had my rifle as a last resource, but I did not wish to spoil his royal hide, so I galloped back to the camp and returned with a cowboy and a fresh lasso. We threw to our victim a stick of wood which he seized in his teeth, and before he could relinquish it our lassoes whistled through the air and tightened on his neck.

Yet before the light had died from his fierce eyes, I cried, 'Stay, we will not kill him; let us take him alive to the camp.' He was so completely powerless now that it was easy to put a stout stick through his mouth, behind his tusks, and then lash his jaws with a heavy cord which was also fastened to the stick. The stick kept the cord in, and the cord kept the stick in so he was harmless. As soon as he felt his jaws were tied he made no further resistance, and uttered no sound, but looked calmly at us and seemed to say, 'Well, you have got me at last, do as you please with me.' And from that time he took no more notice of us.

We tied his feet securely, but he never groaned, nor growled, nor turned his head. Then with our united strength were just able to put him on my horse. His breath came evenly as though sleeping, and his eyes were bright and clear again, but did not rest on us. Afar on the great rolling mesas they were fixed, his passing kingdom, where his famous band was now scattered. And he gazed till the pony descended the pathway into the cañon, and the rocks cut off the view.

By travelling slowly we reached the ranch in safety, and after securing him with a collar and a strong chain, we staked him out in the pasture and removed the cords. Then for the first time I could examine him closely, and proved how unreliable is vulgar report when a living hero or tyrant is concerned. He had *not* a collar of gold about his neck, nor was there on his shoulders an inverted cross to denote that he had leagued himself with Satan. But I did find on one haunch a great broad scar, that tradition says was the fang-mark of Juno, the leader of Tannerey's wolf-hounds – a mark which she gave him the moment before he stretched her lifeless on the sand of the cañon.

I set meat and water beside him, but he paid no heed. He lay calmly on his breast, and gazed with those steadfast yellow eyes away past me down through the gateway of the cañon, over the open plains – his plains – nor moved a muscle when I touched him. When the sun went down he was still gazing fixedly across the prairie. I expected he would call up his band when night came, and prepared for them, but he had called once in his extremity, and none had come; he would never call again.

A lion shorn of his strength, an eagle robbed of his freedom, or a dove bereft of his mate, all die, it is said, of a broken heart; and who will aver that this grim bandit could bear the threefold brunt, heart-whole? This only I know, that when the morning dawned, he was lying there still in his position of calm repose, his body unwounded, but his spirit was gone – the old King-wolf was dead.

I took the chain from his neck, a cowboy helped me to carry him to the shed where lay the remains of Blanca, and as we laid him beside her, the cattle-man exclaimed: 'There, you *would* come to her, now you are together again.'

Badlands Billy

The Wolf that Won

I

THE HOWL BY NIGHT

Do you know the three calls of the hunting Wolf: – the long-drawn deep howl, the muster, that tells of game discovered but too strong for the finder to manage alone; and the higher ululation that ringing and swelling is the cry of the pack on a hot scent; and the sharp bark coupled with a short howl that, seeming least of all, is yet a gong of doom, for this is the cry '*Close in*' – this is the finish?

We were riding the Badland Buttes, King and I, with a pack of various hunting Dogs stringing behind or trotting alongside. The sun had gone from the sky, and a blood-streak marked the spot where he died, away over Sentinel Butte. The hills were dim, the valleys dark, when from the nearest gloom there rolled a long-drawn cry that all men recognize instinctively – melodious, yet with a tone in it that sends a shudder up the spine, though now it has lost all menace for mankind. We listened for a moment. It was the Wolf-hunter who broke silence: 'That's Badlands Billy; ain't it a voice? He's out for his beef tonight.'

II
ANCIENT DAYS

In pristine days the Buffalo herds were followed by bands of Wolves that preyed on the sick, the weak, and the wounded. When the Buffalo were exterminated the Wolves were hard put for support, but the Cattle came and solved the question for them by taking the Buffaloes' place. This caused the wolf-war. The ranchmen offered a bounty for each Wolf killed, and every cowboy out of work, was supplied with traps and poison for wolf-killing. The very expert made this their sole business and became known as wolvers. King Ryder was one of these. He was a quiet, gentle-spoken fellow, with a keen eye and an insight into animal life that gave him especial power over Broncos and Dogs, as well as Wolves and Bears, though in the last two cases it was power merely to surmise where they were and how best to get at them. He had been a wolver for years, and greatly surprised me by saying that 'never in all his experience had he known a Grey-wolf to attack a human being'.

We had many camp-fire talks while the other men were sleeping, and then it was I learned the little that he knew about Badlands Billy. 'Six times have I seen him and the seventh will be Sunday, you bet. He takes his long rest then.' And thus on the very ground where it all fell out, to the noise of the night wind and the yapping of the Coyote, interrupted sometimes by the deep-drawn howl of the hero himself, I heard chapters of this history which, with others gleaned in many fields, gave me the story of the Big Dark Wolf of Sentinel Butte.

III
IN THE CAÑON

Away back in the spring of '92 a wolver was 'wolving' on the east side of the Sentinel Mountain that so long was a principal landmark of the old Plainsmen. Pelts were not good in May, but the bounties were high, five dollars a head, and double for She-wolves. As he went down to the creek one morning he saw a Wolf coming to drink on the other side. He had an easy shot, and on killing it found it was a nursing She-wolf. Evidently her family were somewhere near, so he spent two or three days searching in all the likely places, but found no clue to the den.

Two weeks afterwards, as the wolver rode down an adjoining cañon, he saw a Wolf come out of a hole. The ever-ready rifle flew up, and another ten-dollar scalp was added to his string. Now he dug into the den and found the litter, a most surprising one indeed, for it consisted not of the usual five or six Wolf-pups, but of eleven, and these, strange to say, were of two sizes, five of them larger and older than the other six. Here were two distinct families with one mother, and as he added their scalps to his string of trophies the truth dawned on the hunter. One lot was surely the family of the She-wolf he had killed two weeks before. The case was clear: the little ones awaiting the mother that was never to come, had whined piteously and more loudly as their hunger-pangs increased; the other mother passing had heard the Cubs; her heart was tender now, her own little ones had so recently come, and she cared for the orphans, carried them to her own den, and was providing for the double family when the rifleman had cut the gentle chapter short.

Many a wolver has dug into a wolf-den to find nothing.

The old Wolves or possibly the Cubs themselves often dig little side pockets and off galleries, and when an enemy is breaking in they hide in these. The loose earth conceals the small pocket and thus the Cubs escape. When the wolver retired with his scalps he did not know that the biggest of all the Cubs, was still in the den, and even had he waited about for two hours, he might have been no wiser. Three hours later the sun went down and there was a slight scratching afar in the hole; first two little grey paws, then a small black nose appeared in a soft sand-pile to one side of the den. At length the Cub came forth from his hiding. He had been frightened by the attack on the den; now he was perplexed by its condition.

It was thrice as large as it had been and open at the top now. Lying near were things that smelled like his brothers and sisters, but they were repellent to him. He was filled with fear as he sniffed at them, and sneaked aside into a thicket of grass, as a Night-hawk boomed over his head. He crouched all night in that thicket. He did not dare to go near the den, and knew not where else he could go. The next morning when two Vultures came swooping down on the bodies, the Wolf-cub ran off in the thicket, and seeking its deepest cover, was led down a ravine to a wide valley. Suddenly there arose from the grass a big She-wolf, like his mother, yet different, a stranger, and instinctively the stray Cub sank to the earth, as the old Wolf bounded on him. No doubt the Cub had been taken for some lawful prey, but a whiff set that right. She stood over him for an instant. He grovelled at her feet. The impulse to kill him or at least give him a shake died away. He had the smell of a young Cub. Her own were about his age, her heart was touched, and when he found courage enough to put his nose up and smell her nose, she made no angry demonstration except a short half-hearted growl. Now, however, he had smelled something that he sorely needed. He had not fed since the day before, and when the old Wolf turned to leave him, he tumbled after her on clumsy puppy legs. Had the Mother-wolf been far from home he must soon have been left behind, but the nearest hollow was the chosen place, and the Cub arrived at the den's mouth soon after the Mother-wolf.

A stranger is an enemy, and the old one rushing forth to the defence, met the Cub again, and again was restrained by something that rose in her responsive to the smell. The Cub had thrown himself on his back in utter submission, but that did not prevent his nose reporting to him the good thing almost within reach. The She-wolf went into the den and curled herself about her brood; the Cub persisted in following. She snarled as he approached her own little ones, but disarming wrath each time by submission and his very cubhood, he was presently among her brood, helping himself to what he wanted so greatly, and thus he adopted himself into her family. In a few days he was so much one of them that the mother forgot about his being a stranger. Yet he was different from them in several ways – older by two weeks, stronger, and marked on the neck and shoulders with what afterwards grew to be a dark mane.

Little Duskymane could not have been happier in his choice of a foster-mother, for the Yellow Wolf was not only a good hunter with a fund of cunning, but she was a Wolf of modern ideas as well. The old tricks of tolling a Prairie Dog, relaying for Antelope, houghing a Bronco or flanking a Steer she had learned partly from instinct and partly from the example of her more experienced relatives, when they joined to form the winter bands. But, just as necessary nowadays, she had learned that all men carry guns, that guns are irresistible, that the only way to avoid them is by keeping out of sight while the sun is up, and yet that at night they are harmless. She had a fair comprehension of traps, indeed she had been in one once, and though she left a toe behind in pulling free, it was a toe most advantageously disposed of; thenceforth, though not comprehending the nature of the trap, she was thoroughly imbued with the horror of it, with the idea indeed that iron is dangerous, and at any price it should be avoided.

On one occasion, when she and five others were planning to raid a Sheep yard, she held back at the last minute because some new-strung wires appeared. The others rushed in to find the Sheep beyond their reach, themselves in a death-trap.

Thus she had learned the newer dangers, and while it is unlikely that she had any clear mental conception of them she had acquired a wholesome distrust of all things strange, and a horror of one or two in particular that proved her lasting safeguard. Each year she raised her brood successfully and the number of Yellow Wolves increased in the country. Guns, traps, men and the new animals they brought had been learned, but there was yet another lesson before her – a terrible one indeed.

About the time Duskymane's brothers were a month old his foster-mother returned in a strange condition. She was frothing at the mouth, her legs trembled, and she fell in a convulsion near the doorway of the den, but recovering, she came in. Her jaws quivered, her teeth rattled a little as she tried to lick the little ones; she seized her own front leg and bit it so as not to bite them, but at length she grew quieter and calmer. The Cubs had retreated in fear to a far pocket, but now they returned and crowded about her to seek their usual food. The mother recovered, but was very ill for two or three days, and those days with the poison in her system worked disaster for the brood. They were terribly sick; only the strongest could survive, and when the trial of strength was over, the den contained only the old one and the Black-maned Cub, the one she had adopted. Thus little Duskymane became her sole charge; all her strength was devoted to feeding him, and he thrived apace.

Wolves are quick to learn certain things. The reactions of smell are the greatest that a Wolf can feel, and thenceforth both Cub and foster-mother experienced a quick, unreasoning sense of fear and hate the moment the smell of strychnine reached them.

IV
THE RUDIMENTS OF WOLF TRAINING

With the sustenance of seven at his service the little Wolf had every reason to grow, and when in the autumn he began to follow his mother on her hunting trips he was as tall as she was. Now a change of region was forced on them, for numbers of little Wolves were growing up. Sentinel Butte, the rocky fastness of the plains, was claimed by many that were big and strong; the weaker must move out, and with them Yellow Wolf and the Dusky Cub.

Wolves have no language in the sense that man has; their vocabulary is probably limited to a dozen howls, barks, and grunts expressing the simplest emotions; but they have several other modes of conveying ideas, and one very special method of spreading information – the Wolf-telephone. Scattered over their range are a number of recognized 'centrals'. Sometimes these are stones, sometimes the angle of cross-trails, sometimes a Buffalo-skull – indeed, any conspicuous object near a main trail is used. A Wolf calling here, as a Dog does at a telegraph post, or a Muskrat at a certain mud-pie point, leaves his body-scent and learns what other visitors have been there recently to do the same.

He learns also whence they came and where they went as well as something about their condition, whether hunted, hungry, gorged, or sick. By this system of registration a Wolf knows where his friends, as well as his foes, are to be found. And Duskymane, following after the Yellow Wolf, was taught the places and uses of the many signal-stations without any conscious attempt at teaching on the part of his foster-mother. Example backed by his native instincts was indeed the chief teacher, but on one occasion at least there was something very like the effort of a human parent to guard her child in danger.

The Dark Cub had learned the rudiments of Wolf life: that the way to fight Dogs is to run, and to fight as you run, never grapple, but snap, snap, snap, and make for the rough country where Horses cannot bring their riders.

He learned not to bother about the Coyotes that follow for the pickings when you hunt; you cannot catch them and they do you no harm.

He knew he must not waste time dashing after Birds that alight on the ground; and that he must keep away from the little black and white Animal with the bushy tail. It is not very good to eat, and it is very, very bad to smell.

Poison! Oh, he never forgot that smell from the day when the den was cleared of all his foster-brothers.

He now knew that the first move in attacking Sheep was to scatter them; a lone Sheep is a foolish and easy prey; that the way to round up a band of Cattle was to frighten a Calf.

He learned that he must always attack a Steer behind, a Sheep in front, and a Horse in the middle, that is, on the flank, and never, never attack a man at all, never even face him. But an important lesson was added to these, one in which the mother consciously taught him of a secret foe.

V
THE LESSON ON TRAPS

A Calf had died in branding-time and now, two weeks later, was in its best state for perfect taste, not too fresh, not over-ripe – that is, in a Wolf's opinion – and the wind carried this information afar. The Yellow Wolf and Duskymane were out for supper, though not yet knowing where, when the tidings of veal arrived, and they trotted up the wind. The Calf was in an open place, and plain to be seen in the moonlight. A Dog would have trotted right up to the carcass, an old-time Wolf might have done so, but constant war had developed constant vigilance in the Yellow Wolf, and trusting nothing and no one but her nose, she slacked her speed to a walk. On coming in easy view she stopped, and for long swung her nose, submitting the wind to the closest possible chemical analysis. She tried it with her finest tests, blew all the membranes clean again and tried it once more; and this was the report of the trusty nostrils, yes, the unanimous report. First, rich and racy smell of Calf, seventy per cent.; smells of grass, bugs, wood, flowers, trees, sand, and other uninteresting negations, fifteen per cent.; smell of her Cub and herself, positive but ignorable, ten per cent.; smell of human tracks, two per cent.; smell of smoke, one per cent.; of sweaty leather smell, one per cent.; of human body-scent (not discernible in some samples), one-half per cent.; smell of iron, a trace.

The old Wolf crouched a little but sniffed hard with swinging nose; the young Wolf imitatively did the same. She backed off to a greater distance; the Cub stood. She gave a low whine; he followed unwillingly. She circled around the tempting carcass; a new smell was recorded – Coyote trail-scent, soon followed by Coyote body-scent.

Yes, there they were sneaking along a near ridge, and now as she passed to one side the samples changed, the wind had lost nearly every trace of Calf; miscellaneous, commonplace, and uninteresting smells were there instead. The human track-scent was as before, the trace of leather was gone, but fully one-half per cent. of iron-odour, and body-smell of man raised to nearly two per cent.

Fully alarmed, she conveyed her fear to the Cub, by her rigid pose, her air intent, and her slightly bristling mane.

She continued her round. At one time on a high place the human body-scent was doubly strong, then as she dropped it faded. Then the wind brought the full calf-odour with several track-scents of Coyotes and sundry Birds. Her suspicions were lulling as in a smalling circle she neared the tempting feast from the windward side. She had even advanced straight towards it for a few steps when the sweaty leather sang loud and strong again, and smoke and iron mingled like two strands of a parti-coloured yarn. Centring all her attention on this, she advanced within two leaps of the Calf. There on the ground was a scrap of leather, telling also of a human touch, close at hand the Calf, and now the iron and smoke on the full vast smell of Calf were like a Snake trail across the trail of a whole Beef herd. It was so slight that the Cub, with the appetite and impatience of youth, pressed up against his mother's shoulder to go past and eat without delay. She seized him by the neck and flung him back. A stone struck by his feet rolled forward and stopped with a peculiar clink. The danger smell was greatly increased at this, and the Yellow Wolf backed slowly from the feast, the Cub unwillingly following.

As he looked wistfully he saw the Coyotes drawing nearer, mindful chiefly to avoid the Wolves. He watched their really cautious advance; it seemed like heedless rushing compared with his mother's approach. The Calf smell rolled forth in exquisite and overpowering excellence now, for they were tearing the meat, when a sharp clank was heard and a yelp from a Coyote. At the same time the quiet night was shocked with a roar and a flash of fire. Heavy shots spattered Calf and Coyotes, and yelping like beaten Dogs they scattered, excepting one that was killed and a second struggling in the trap set here by the ever-active wolvers. The air was charged with the hateful smells redoubled now, and horrid smells additional. The Yellow Wolf glided down a hollow and led her Cub away in flight, but, as they went, they saw a man rush from the bank near where the mother's nose had warned her of the human scent. They saw him kill the caught Coyote and set the traps for more.

VI

THE BEGUILING OF THE YELLOW WOLF

The life game is a hard game, for we may win ten thousand times, and if we fail but once our gain is gone. How many hundred times had the Yellow Wolf scorned the traps; how many Cubs she had trained to do the same! Of all the dangers to her life she best knew traps.

October had come; the Cub was now much taller than the mother. The wolver had seen them once – a Yellow Wolf followed by another, whose long, awkward legs, big, soft feet, thin neck, and skimpy tail proclaimed him this year's Cub. The record of the dust and sand said that the old one had lost a right front toe, and that the young one was of giant size.

It was the wolver that thought to turn the carcass of the Calf to profit, but he was disappointed in getting Coyotes instead of Wolves. It was the beginning of the trapping season, for this month fur is prime. A young trapper often fastens the bait on the trap; an experienced one does not. A good trapper will even put the bait at one place and the trap ten or twenty feet away, but at a spot that the Wolf is likely to cross in circling. A favourite plan is to hide three or four traps around an open place, and scatter some scraps of meat in the middle. The traps are buried out of sight after being smoked to hide the taint of hands and iron. Sometimes no bait is used except a little piece of cotton or a tuft of feathers that may catch the Wolf's eye or pique its curiosity and tempt it to circle on the fateful, treacherous ground. A good trapper varies his methods continually so that the Wolves cannot learn his ways. Their only safeguards are perpetual vigilance and distrust of all smells that are known to be of man.

The wolver, with a load of the strongest steel traps, had begun his autumn work on the 'Cottonwood'.

An old Buffalo trail crossing the river followed a little draw that climbed the hills to the level upland. All animals use these trails, Wolves and Foxes as well as Cattle and Deer: they are the main thoroughfares. A cottonwood stump not far from where it plunged to the gravelly stream was marked with Wolf signs that told the wolver of its use. Here was an excellent place for traps, not on the trail, for Cattle were here in numbers, but twenty yards away on a level, sandy spot he set four traps in a twelve-foot square. Near each he scattered two or three scraps of meat; three or four white feathers on a spear of grass in the middle completed the setting. No human eye, few animal noses, could have detected the hidden danger of that sandy ground, when the sun and wind and the sand itself had dissipated the man-track taint.

The Yellow Wolf had seen and passed, and taught her giant son to pass, such traps a thousand times before.

The Cattle came to water in the heat of the day. They strung down the Buffalo path as once the Buffalo did. The little Vesper-birds flitted before them, the Cowbirds rode on them, and the Prairie-dogs chattered at them, just as they once did at the Buffalo.

Down from the grey-green mesa with its green-grey rocks, they marched with imposing solemnity, importance, and directness of purpose. Some frolicsome Calves, playing alongside the trail, grew sober and walked behind their mothers as the river flat was reached. The old Cow that headed the procession sniffed suspiciously as she passed the 'trap set', but it was far away, otherwise she would have pawed and bellowed over the scraps of bloody beef till every trap was sprung and harmless.

But she led to the river. After all had drunk their fill they lay down on the nearest bank till late afternoon. Then their unheard dinner-gong aroused them, and started them on the backward march to where the richest pastures grew.

One or two small birds had picked at the scraps of meat, some blue-bottle flies buzzed about, but the sinking sun saw the sandy mask untouched.

A brown Marsh Hawk came skimming over the river flat as the sun began his colour play. Blackbirds dashed into thickets, and easily avoided his clumsy pounce. It was too early for the Mice, but, as he skimmed the ground, his keen eye caught the flutter of feathers by the trap and turned his flight. The feathers in their uninteresting emptiness were exposed before he was near, but now he saw the scraps of meat. Guileless of cunning, he alighted and was devouring a second lump when – *clank* – the dust was flirted high and the Marsh Hawk was held by his toes, struggling vainly in the jaws of a powerful wolf-trap. He was not much hurt. His ample wings winnowed from time to time, in efforts to be free, but he was helpless, even as a Sparrow might be in a rat-trap, and when the sun had played his fierce chromatic scale, his swan-song sung, and died as he dies only in the blazing west, and the shades had fallen on the melodramatic scene of the Mouse in the elephant-trap, there was a deep, rich sound on the high flat butte, answered by another, neither very long, neither repeated, and both instinctive rather than necessary. One was the muster-call of an ordinary Wolf, the other the answer of a very big male, not a pair in this case, but mother and son – Yellow Wolf and Duskymane. They came trotting together down the Buffalo trail. They paused at the telephone box on the hill and again at the old cottonwood root, and were making for the river when the Hawk in the trap fluttered his wings. The old Wolf turned towards him – a wounded bird on the ground surely, and she rushed forward. Sun and sand soon burn all trail-scents; there was nothing to warn her. She sprang on the flopping bird and a chop of her jaws ended his troubles, but a horrid sound – the gritting of her teeth on steel – told her of peril. She dropped the Hawk and sprang backward from the dangerous ground, but landed in the second trap. High on her foot its death-grip closed, and leaping with all her strength, to escape, she set her fore foot in another of the lurking grips of steel. Never had a trap been so baited before. Never was she so unsuspicious. Never was catch more sure. Fear and fury filled the old Wolf's heart; she tugged and strained, she chewed the chains, she snarled and foamed. One trap with its buried log, she might have dragged; with two, she was helpless. Struggle as she might, it only worked those relentless jaws more deeply into her feet. She snapped wildly at the air; she tore the dead Hawk into shreds; she roared the short, barking roar of a crazy Wolf. She bit at the traps, at her Cub, at herself. She tore her legs that were held; she gnawed in frenzy at her flank, she chopped off her tail in her madness; she splintered all her teeth on the steel, and filled her bleeding, foaming jaws with clay and sand.

She struggled till she fell, and writhed about or lay like dead, till strong enough to rise and grind the chains again with her teeth.

And so the night passed by.

And Duskymane? Where was he? The feeling of the time when his foster-mother had come home poisoned, now returned; but he was even more afraid of her. She seemed filled with fighting hate. He held away and whined a little; he slunk off and came back when she lay still, only to retreat again, as she sprang forward, raging at him, and then renewed her efforts at the traps. He did not understand it, but he knew this much, she was in terrible trouble, and the cause seemed to be the same as that which had scared them the night they had ventured near the Calf.

Duskymane hung about all night, fearing to go near, not knowing what to do, and helpless as his mother.

At dawn the next day a sheepherder seeking lost Sheep discovered her from a neighbouring hill. A signal mirror called the wolver from his camp. Duskymane saw the new danger. He was a mere Cub, though so tall; he could not face the man, and fled at his approach.

The wolver rode up to the sorry, tattered, bleeding She-wolf in the trap. He raised his rifle and soon the struggling stopped.

The wolver read the trail and the signs about, and remembering those he had read before, he divined that this was the Wolf with the great Cub – the She-wolf of Sentinel Butte.

Duskymane heard the 'crack' as he scurried off into cover. He could scarcely know what it meant, but he never saw his kind old foster-mother again. Thenceforth he must face the world alone.

VII

THE YOUNG WOLF WINS A PLACE AND FAME

Instinct is no doubt a Wolf's first and best guide, but gifted parents are a great start in life. The dusky-maned Cub had had a mother of rare excellence and he reaped the advantage of all her cleverness. He had inherited an exquisite nose and had absolute confidence in its admonitions. Mankind has difficulty in recognizing the power of nostrils. A Grey-wolf can glance over the morning wind as a man does over his newspaper, and get all the latest news. He can swing over the ground and have the minutest information of every living creature that has walked there within many hours. His nose even tells which way it ran, and in a word renders a statement of every animal that recently crossed his trail, whence it came, and whither it went.

That power had Duskymane in the highest degree; his broad, moist nose was evidence of it to all who are judges of such things. Added to this, his frame was of unusual power and endurance, and last, he had early learned a deep distrust of everything strange, and, call it what we will, shyness, wariness or suspicion, it was worth more to him than all his cleverness. It was this as much as his physical powers that made a success of his life. Might is right in wolf-land, and Duskymane and his mother had been driven out of Sentinel Butte. But it was a very delectable land and he kept drifting back to his native mountain. One or two big Wolves there resented his coming. They drove him off several times, yet each time he returned he was better able to face them; and before he was eighteen months old he had defeated all rivals and established himself again on his native ground; where he lived like a robber baron, levying tribute on the rich lands about him and finding safety in the rocky fastness.

Wolver Ryder often hunted in that country, and before long, he came across a five-and-one-half-inch track, the foot-print of a giant Wolf. Roughly reckoned, twenty to twenty-five pounds of weight or six inches of stature is a fair allowance for each inch of a Wolf's foot; this Wolf therefore stood thirty-three inches at the shoulder and weighed about one hundred and forty pounds, by far the largest Wolf he had ever met. King had lived in Goat country, and now in Goat language he exclaimed: 'You bet, ain't that an old Billy?' Thus by trivial chance it was that Duskymane was known to his foe, as 'Badlands Billy'.

Ryder was familiar with the muster-call of the Wolves, the long, smooth cry, but Billy's had a singular feature, a slurring that was always distinctive. Ryder had heard this before, in the Cottonwood Cañon, and when at length he got a sight of the big Wolf with the black mane, it struck him that this was also the Cub of the old Yellow fury that he had trapped.

These were among the things he told me as we sat by the fire at night. I knew of the early days when any one could trap or poison Wolves, of the passing of those days, with the passing of the simple Wolves; of the new race of Wolves with new cunning that were defying the methods of the ranchmen, and increasing steadily in numbers. Now the wolver told me of the various ventures that Penroof had made with different kinds of Hounds: of Foxhounds too thin-skinned to fight; of Greyhounds that were useless when the animal was out of sight; of Danes too heavy for the rough country, and, last, of the composite pack with some of all kinds, including at times a Bull-terrier to lead them in the final fight.

He told of hunts after Coyotes, which usually were successful because the Coyotes sought the plains, and were easily caught by the Greyhounds. He told of killing some small Grey-wolves with this very pack, usually at the cost of the one that led them; but above all he dwelt on the wonderful prowess of 'that thar cussed old Black Wolf of Sentinel Butte', and related the many attempts to run him down or corner him – an unbroken array of failures. For the big Wolf, with exasperating persistence, continued to live on the finest stock of the Penroof brand, and each year was teaching more Wolves how to do the same with perfect impunity.

I listened even as gold-hunters listen to stories of treasure trove, for these were the things of my world. These things indeed were uppermost in all our minds, for the Penroof pack was lying around our camp-fire now. We were out after Badlands Billy.

VIII

THE VOICE IN THE NIGHT AND THE BIG TRACK IN THE MORNING

One night late in September after the last streak of light was gone from the west and the Coyotes had begun their yapping chorus, a deep, booming sound was heard. King took out his pipe, turned his head and said: 'That's him – that's old Billy. He's been watching us all day from some high place, and now when the guns are useless he's here to have a little fun with us.'

Two or three Dogs arose, with bristling manes, for they clearly recognized that this was no Coyote. They rushed out into the night, but did not go far; their brawling sounds were suddenly varied by loud yelps, and they came running back to the shelter of the fire. One was so badly cut in the shoulder that he was useless for the rest of the hunt. Another was hurt in the flank – it seemed the less serious wound, and yet next morning the hunters buried that second Dog.

The men were furious. They vowed speedy vengeance, and at dawn were off on the trail. The Coyotes yelped their dawning song, but they melted into the hills when the light was strong. The hunters searched about for the big Wolf's track, hoping that the Hounds would be able to take it up and find him, but they either could not or would not.

They found a Coyote, however, and within a few hundred yards they killed him. It was a victory, I suppose, for Coyotes kill Calves and Sheep, but somehow I felt the common thought of all: 'Mighty brave Dogs for a little Coyote, but they could not face the big Wolf last night.'

Young Penroof, as though in answer to one of the unput questions, said:

'Say, boys, I believe old Billy had a hull bunch of Wolves with him last night.'

'Didn't see but one track,' said King gruffly.

In this way the whole of October slipped by; all day hard riding after doubtful trails, following the Dogs, who either could not keep the big trail or feared to do so, and again and again we had news of damage done by the Wolf; sometimes a cowboy would report it to us; and sometimes we found the carcasses ourselves. A few of these we poisoned, though it is considered a very dangerous thing to do while running Dogs. The end of the month found us a weather-beaten, dispirited lot of men, with a worn-out lot of Horses, and a foot-sore pack, reduced in numbers from ten to seven. So far we had killed only one Grey-wolf and three Coyotes; Badlands Billy had killed at least a dozen Cows and Dogs at fifty dollars a head. Some of the boys decided to give it up and go home, so King took advantage of their going, to send a letter, asking for reinforcements including all the spare Dogs at the ranch.

During the two days' wait we rested our Horses, shot some game, and prepared for a harder hunt. Late on the second day the new Dogs arrived – eight beauties – and raised the working pack to fifteen.

The weather now turned much cooler, and in the morning, to the joy of the wolvers, the ground was white with snow. This surely meant success. With cool weather for the Dogs and Horses to run; with the big Wolf not far away, for he had been heard the night before; and with tracking snow, so that once found he could not baffle us – escape for him was impossible.

We were up at dawn, but before we could get away, three men came riding into camp. They were the Penroof boys back again. The change of weather had changed their minds; they knew that with snow we might have luck.

'Remember now,' said King, as all were mounting, 'we don't want any but Badlands Billy this trip. Get him an' we kin bust up the hull combination. It is a five-and-a-half-inch track.'

And each measured off on his quirt handle, or on his glove, the exact five and a half inches that was to be used in testing the tracks he might find.

Not more than an hour elapsed before we got a signal from the rider who had gone westward. One shot: that means 'attention', a pause while counting ten, then two shots: that means '*come on*'.

King gathered the Dogs and rode direct to the distant figure on the hill. All hearts beat high with hope, and we were not disappointed. Some small Wolf tracks had been found, but here at last was the big track, nearly six inches long. Young Penroof wanted to yell and set out at full gallop. It was like hunting a Lion; it was like finding happiness long deferred. The hunter knows nothing more inspiring than the clean-cut line of fresh tracks that is leading to a wonderful animal, he has long been hunting in vain. How King's eye gleamed as he gloated over the sign!

IX
RUN DOWN AT LAST

It was the roughest of all rough riding. It was a far longer hunt than we had expected, and was full of little incidents, for that endless line of marks was a minute history of all that the big Wolf had done the night before. Here he had circled at the telephone box and looked for news; there he had paused to examine an old skull; here he had shied off and swung cautiously up wind to examine something that proved to be an old tin can; there at length he had mounted a low hill and sat down, probably giving the muster-howl, for two Wolves had come to him from different directions, and they then had descended to the river flat where the Cattle would seek shelter during the storm. Here all three had visited a Buffalo skull; there they trotted in line; and yonder they separated, going three different ways, to meet – yes – here – oh, what a sight, a fine Cow ripped open, left dead and *uneaten*. Not to their taste, it seems, for see! within a mile is another killed by them. Not six hours ago, they had feasted. Here their trails scatter again, but not far, and the snow tells plainly how each had lain down to sleep. The Hounds' manes bristled as they sniffed those places. King had held the Dogs well in hand, but now they were greatly excited. We came to a hill whereon the Wolves had turned and faced our way, then fled at full speed – so said the trail – and now it was clear that they had watched us from that hill, and were not far away.

The pack kept well together, because the Greyhounds,

seeing no quarry, were merely puttering about among the other Dogs, or running back with the Horses. We went as fast as we could, for the Wolves were speeding. Up mesas and down coulees we rode, sticking closely to the Dogs, though it was the roughest country that could be picked. One gully after another, an hour and another hour, and still the threefold track went bounding on; another hour and no change, but interminable climbing, sliding, struggling, through brush and over boulders, guided by the far-away yelping of the Dogs.

Now the chase led downward to the low valley of the river, where there was scarcely any snow. Jumping and scrambling down hills, recklessly leaping dangerous gullies and slippery rocks, we felt that we could not hold out much longer; when on the lowest, dryest level the pack split, some went up, some went down, and others straight on. Oh, how King did swear! He knew at once what it meant. The Wolves had scattered, and so had divided the pack. Three Dogs after a Wolf would have no chance, four could not kill him, two would certainly be killed. And yet this was the first encouraging sign we had seen, for it meant that the Wolves were hard pressed. We spurred ahead to stop the Dogs, to pick for them the only trail. But that was not so easy. Without snow here and with countless Dog tracks, we were foiled. All we could do was to let the Dogs choose, but keep them to a single choice. Away we went as before, hoping, yet fearing that we were not on the right track. The Dogs ran well, very fast indeed. This was a bad sign, King said, but we could not get sight of the track because the Dogs overran it before we came.

After a two-mile run the chase led upward again in snow country; the Wolf was sighted, but to our disgust, we were on the track of the smallest one.

'I thought so,' growled young Penroof. 'Dogs was

altogether too keen for a serious proposition. Kind o' surprised it ain't turned out a Jack-rabbit.'

Within another mile he had turned to bay in a willow thicket. We heard him howl the long-drawn howl for help, and before we could reach the place King saw the Dogs recoil and scatter. A minute later there sped from the far side of the thicket a small Grey-wolf and a Black One of very much greater size.

'By golly, if he didn't yell for help, and Billy come back to help him; that's great!' exclaimed the wolver. And my heart went out to the brave old Wolf that refused to escape by abandoning his friend.

The next hour was a hard repetition of the gully riding, but it was on the highlands where there was snow, and when again the pack was split, we strained every power and succeeded in keeping them on the big 'five-fifty track', that already was wearing for me the glamour of romance.

Evidently the Dogs preferred either of the others, but we got them going at last. Another half hour's hard work and far ahead, as I rose to a broad flat plain, I had my first glimpse of the Big Black Wolf of Sentinel Butte.

'Hurrah! Badlands Billy! Hurrah! Badlands Billy!' I shouted in salute, and the others took up the cry.

We were on his track at last, thanks to himself. The Dogs joined in with a louder baying, the Greyhounds yelped and made straight for him, and the Horses sniffed and sprang more gamely as they caught the thrill. The only silent one was the black-maned Wolf, and as I marked his size and power, and above all his long and massive jaws, I knew why the Dogs preferred some other trail.

With head and tail low he was bounding over the snow. His tongue was lolling long; plainly he was hard pressed. The wolvers' hands flew to their revolvers, though he was three hundred yards ahead; they were out for blood, not sport. But an instant later he had sunk from view in the nearest sheltered cañon.

Now which way would he go, up or down the cañon? Up was towards his mountain, down was better cover. King and I thought 'up', so pressed westward along the ridge. But the others rode eastward, watching for a chance to shoot.

Soon we had ridden out of hearing. We were wrong – the Wolf had gone down, but we heard no shooting. The cañon was crossable here; we reached the other side and then turned back at a gallop, scanning the snow for a trail, the hills for a moving form, or the wind for a sound of life.

'Squeak, squeak,' went our saddle leathers, 'puff – puff' our Horses, and their feet 'ka-ka-lump, ka-ka-lump'.

X

WHEN BILLY WENT BACK TO HIS MOUNTAIN

We were back opposite to where the Wolf had plunged, but saw no sign. We rode at an easy gallop, on eastward, a mile, and still on, when King gasped out, 'Look at that!' A dark spot was moving on the snow ahead. We put on speed. Another dark spot appeared, and another, but they were not going fast. In five minutes we were near them, to find – three of our own Greyhounds. They had lost sight of the game, and with that their interest waned. Now they were seeking us. We saw nothing there of the chase or of the other hunters. But hastening to the next ridge we stumbled on the trail we sought and followed as hard as though in view. Another cañon came in our path, and as we rode and looked for a place to cross, a wild din of Hounds came from its brushy depth. The clamour grew and passed up the middle.

We raced along the rim, hoping to see the game. The Dogs appeared near the farther side, not in a pack, but a long, straggling line. In five minutes more they rose to the edge, and ahead of them was the great Black Wolf. He was loping as before, head and tail low. Power was plain in every limb, and double power in his jaws and neck, but I thought his bounds were shorter now, and that they had lost their spring. The Dogs slowly reached the upper level, and sighting him they broke into a feeble cry; they, too, were nearly spent. The Greyhounds saw the chase, and leaving us they scrambled down the cañon and up the other side at impetuous speed that would surely break them down, while we rode, vainly seeking means of crossing.

How the wolver raved to see the pack lead off in the climax of the chase, and himself held up behind. But he rode and wrathed and still rode, up to where the cañon dwindled – rough land and a hard ride. As we neared the great flat mountain, the feeble cry of the pack was heard again from the south, then towards the high Butte's side, and just a trifle louder now. We reined in on a hillock and scanned the snow. A moving speck appeared, then others, not bunched, but in a straggling train, and at times there was a far faint cry. They were headed towards us, coming on, yes! coming, but so slowly, for not one was really running now. There was the grim old Cow-killer limping over the ground, and far behind a Greyhound, and another, and farther still, the other Dogs in order of their speed, slowly, gamely, dragging themselves on that pursuit. Many hours of hardest toil had done their work. The Wolf had vainly sought to fling them off. Now was his hour of doom, for he was spent; they still had some reserve. Straight to us for a time they came, skirting the base of the mountain, crawling.

We could not cross to join them, so held our breath and

gazed with ravenous eyes. They were nearer now, the wind brought feeble notes from the Hounds. The big Wolf turned to the steep ascent, up a well-known trail, it seemed, for he made no slip. My heart went with him, for he had come back to rescue his friend, and a momentary thrill of pity came over us both, as we saw him glance around and drag himself up the sloping way, to die on his mountain. There was no escape for him, beset by fifteen Dogs with men to back them. He was not walking, but tottering upward; the Dogs behind in line, were now doing a little better, were nearing him. We could hear them gasping; we scarcely heard them bay – they had no breath for that; upward the grim procession went, circling a spur of the Butte and along a ledge that climbed and narrowed, then dropped for a few yards to a shelf that reared above the cañon. The foremost Dogs were closing, fearless of a foe so nearly spent.

Here in the narrowest place, where one wrong step meant death, the great Wolf turned and faced them. With fore-feet braced, with head low and tail a little raised, his dusky mane a-bristling, his glittering tusks laid bare, but uttering no sound that we could hear, he faced the crew. His legs were weak with toil, but his neck, his jaws, and his heart were strong, and – now all you who love the Dogs had better close the book – on – up and down – fifteen to one, they came, the swiftest first, and how it was done, the eye could scarcely see, but even as a stream of water pours on a rock to be splashed in broken jets aside, that stream of Dogs came pouring down the path, in single file perforce, and Duskymane received them as they came. A feeble spring, a counter-lunge, a gash, and 'Fango's down', has lost his foothold and is gone. Dander and Coalie close and try to clinch; a rush, a heave, and they are fallen from that narrow path. Blue-spot then, backed by mighty Oscar and fearless Tige – but the Wolf is next the rock and the flash of combat clears to show him there alone, the big Dogs gone; the rest close in, the hindmost force the foremost on – down – to their death. Slash, chop and heave, from the swiftest to the biggest, to the last, down – down – he sent them whirling from the ledge to the gaping gulch below, where rocks and snags of trunks were sharp to do their work.

In fifty seconds it was done. The rock had splashed the stream aside – the Penroof pack was all wiped out; and Badlands Billy stood there, alone again on his mountain.

A moment he waited to look for more to come. There were no more, the pack was dead; but waiting he got his breath, then raising his voice for the first time in that fatal scene, he feebly gave a long yell of triumph, and scaling the next low bank, was screened from view in a cañon of Sentinel Butte.

We stared like men of stone. The guns in our hands were forgotten. It was all so quick, so final. We made no move till the Wolf was gone. It was not far to the place: we went on foot to see if any had escaped. Not one was left alive. We could do nothing – we could say nothing.

XI

THE HOWL AT SUNSET

A week later we were riding the upper trail back of the Chimney Pot, King and I. 'The old man is pretty sick of it,' he said. 'He'd sell out if he could. He don't know what's the next move.'

The sun went down beyond Sentinel Butte. It was dusk as we reached the turn that led to Dumont's place, and a deep-toned rolling howl came from the river flat below, followed by a number of higher-pitched howls in answering chorus. We could see nothing, but we listened hard. The song was repeated, the hunting-cry of the Wolves. It faded, the night was stirred by another, the sharp bark and the short howl, the signal 'close in'; a bellow came up, very short, for it was cut short.

And King as he touched his Horse said grimly: 'That's him, he is out with the pack, an' thar goes another Beef.'

Little Warhorse

The History of a Jack-rabbit

I

The Little Warhorse knew practically all the Dogs in town. First, there was a very large brown Dog that had pursued him many times, a Dog that he always got rid of by slipping through a hole in a board fence. Second, there was a small active Dog that could follow through that hole, and him he baffled by leaping a twenty-foot irrigation ditch that had steep sides and a swift current. The Dog could not make this leap. It was 'sure medicine' for that foe, and the boys still call the place 'Old Jacky's Jump'. But there was a Greyhound that could leap better than the Jack, and when he could not follow through a fence, he jumped over it. He tried the Warhorse's mettle more than once, and Jacky only saved himself by his quick dodging, till they got to an Osage hedge, and here the Greyhound had to give it up. Besides these, there was in town a rabble of big and little Dogs that were troublesome, but easily left behind in the open.

In the country there was a Dog at each farm-house, but only one that the Warhorse really feared; that was a long-legged, fierce, black Dog, a brute so swift and pertinacious that he had several times forced the Warhorse almost to the last extremity.

For the town Cats he cared little; only once or twice had he been threatened by them. A huge Tom-cat flushed with many victories came crawling up to where he fed one moonlight night. Jack Warhorse saw the black creature with the glowing eyes, and a moment before the final rush, he faced it, raised up on his haunches – his hind legs – at full length on his toes – with his broad ears towering up yet six inches higher; then letting out a loud *churrr-churrr*, his best attempt at a roar, he sprang five feet forward and landed on the Cat's head, driving in his sharp hind nails, and the old Tom fled in terror from the weird two-legged giant. This trick he had tried several times with success, but twice it turned out a sad failure: once, when the Cat proved to be a mother whose Kittens were near; then Jack Warhorse had to flee for his life; and the other time was when he made the mistake of landing hard on a Skunk.

But the Greyhound was the dangerous enemy, and in him the Warhorse might have found his fate, but for a curious adventure with a happy ending for Jack.

He fed by night; there were fewer enemies about then, and it was easier to hide; but one day at dawn in winter he had lingered long at an alfalfa stack and was crossing the open snow towards his favourite form, when, as ill-luck would have it, he met the Greyhound prowling outside the town. With open snow and growing daylight there was no chance to hide, nothing but a run in the open with soft snow that hindered the Jack more than it did the Hound.

Off they went – superb runners in fine fettle. How they skimmed across the snow, raising it in little *puff – puff – puffs*, each time their nimble feet went down. This way and that, swerving and dodging, went the chase. Everything favoured the Dog – his empty stomach, the cold weather, the soft snow – while the Rabbit was handicapped by his heavy meal of alfalfa. But his feet went *puff–puff* so fast that a dozen of the little snowjets were in view at once. The chase continued in the open; no friendly hedge was near, and every attempt to reach a fence was cleverly stopped by the Hound. Jack's ears were losing their bold up-cock, a sure sign of failing heart or wind, when all at once these flags went stiffly up, as under sudden renewal of strength. The Warhorse put forth all his power, not to reach the hedge to the north, but over the open prairie eastward. The Greyhound followed, and within fifty yards the Jack dodged to foil his fierce pursuer; but on the next tack he was on his eastern course again, and so tacking and dodging, he kept the line direct for the next farm-house, where was a very high board fence with a hen-hole, and where also there dwelt his other hated enemy, the big black Dog. An outer hedge delayed the Greyhound for a moment and gave Jack time to dash through the hen-hole into the yard, where he hid to one side. The Greyhound rushed around to the low gate, leaped over that among the Hens, and as they fled cackling and fluttering, some Lambs bleated loudly. Their natural guardian, the big black Dog, ran to the rescue, and Warhorse slipped out again by the hole at which he had entered. Horrible sounds of Dog hate and fury were heard behind him in the hen-yard, and soon the shouts of men were added. How it ended he did not know or seek to learn, but it was remarkable that he never afterwards was troubled by the swift Greyhound that formerly lived in Newchusen.

II

Hard times and easy times had long followed in turn and been taken as matters of course; but recent years in the

State of Kaskado had brought to the Jack-rabbits a succession of remarkable ups and downs. In the old days they had their endless fight with Birds and Beasts of Prey, with cold and heat, with pestilence and with flies whose sting bred a loathsome disease, and yet had held their own. But the settling of the country by farmers made many changes.

Dogs and guns arriving in numbers reduced the ranks of Coyotes, Foxes, Wolves, Badgers, and Hawks that preyed on the Jack, so that in a few years the Rabbits were multiplied in great swarms; but now Pestilence broke out and swept them away. Only the strongest – the double-seasoned – remained. For a while a Jack-rabbit was a rarity; but during this time another change came in. The Osage-orange hedges planted everywhere afforded a new refuge, and now the safety of a Jack-rabbit was less often his speed than his wits, and the wise ones, when pursued by a Dog or Coyote, would rush to the nearest hedge through a small hole and escape while the enemy sought for a larger one by which to follow. The Coyotes rose to this and developed the trick of the relay chase. In this one Coyote takes one field, another the next, and if the Rabbit attempts the 'hedge-ruse' they work from each side and usually win their prey. The Rabbit remedy for this, is keen eyes to see the second Coyote, avoidance of that field, then good legs to distance the first enemy.

Thus the Jack-rabbits, after being successively numerous, scarce, in myriads, and rare, were now again on the increase, and those which survived, selected by a hundred hard trials, were enabled to flourish where their ancestors could not have outlived a single season.

Their favourite grounds were, not the broad open stretches of the big ranches, but the complicated, much-fenced fields of the farms, where these were so small and close as to be like a big straggling village.

One of these vegetable villages had sprung up around the railway station of Newchusen. The country a mile away was well supplied with Jack-rabbits of the new and selected stock. Among them was a little lady Rabbit called 'Bright-eyes', from her leading characteristic as she sat grey in the grey brush. She was a good runner, but was especially successful with the fence-play that baffled the Coyotes. She made her nest out in an open pasture, an untouched tract of the ancient prairie. Here her brood were born and raised. One like herself was bright-eyed, in coat of silver-grey, and partly gifted with her ready wits, but in the other, there appeared a rare combination of his mother's gifts with the best that was in the best strain of the new Jack-rabbits of the plains.

This was the one whose adventures we have been following, the one that later on the turf won the name of Little Warhorse and that afterwards achieved a world-wide fame.

Ancient tricks of his kind he revived and put to new uses, and ancient enemies he learned to fight with new-found tricks.

When a mere baby he discovered a plan that was worthy of the wisest Rabbit in Kaskado. He was pursued by a horrible little Yellow Dog, and he had tried in vain to get rid of him by dodging among the fields and farms. This is good play against a Coyote, because the farmers and the Dogs will often help the Jack, without knowing it, by attacking the Coyote. But now the plan did not work at all, for the little Dog managed to keep after him through one fence after another, and Jack Warhorse, not yet full-grown, much less seasoned, was beginning to feel the strain. His ears were no longer up straight, but angling back and at times drooping to a level, as he darted through a very little hole in an Osage hedge, only to find that his nimble enemy had done the same without loss of time. In the middle of the field was a small herd of Cattle and with them a Calf.

There is in wild animals a curious impulse to trust any stranger when in desperate straits. The foe behind they know means death. There is just a chance, and the only one left, that the stranger may prove friendly; and it was this last desperate chance that drew Jack Warhorse to the Cows.

It is quite sure that the Cows would have stood by in stolid indifference so far as the Rabbit was concerned, but they have a deep-rooted hatred of a Dog, and when they saw the Yellow Cur coming bounding towards them, their tails and noses went up; they sniffed angrily, then closed up ranks, and led by the Cow that owned the Calf, they charged at the Dog, while Jack took refuge under a low thorn-bush. The Dog swerved aside to attack the Calf, at least the old Cow thought he did, and she followed him so fiercely that he barely escaped from that field with his life.

It was a good old plan – one that doubtless came from the days when Buffalo and Coyote played the parts of Cow and Dog. Jack never forgot it, and more than once it saved his life.

In colour as well as in power he was a rarity.

Animals are coloured in one or other of two general plans; one that matches them with their surroundings and helps them to hide – this is called 'protective'; the other that makes them very visible for several purposes – this is called 'directive'. Jack-rabbits are peculiar in being painted both ways. As they squat in their form in the grey brush or clods, they are soft grey on their ears, head, back, and sides; they match the ground and cannot be seen until close at hand – they are *protectively* coloured. But the moment it is clear to the Jack that the approaching foe will find him, he jumps up and dashes away. He throws off all disguise now, the grey seems to disappear; he makes a lightning change, and his ears show snowy white with black tips, the legs are white, his tail is a black spot in a blaze of white. He is a black-and-white Rabbit now. His colouring is all *directive*. How is it done? Very simply. The front side of the ear is grey, the back, black and white. The black tail with its white halo, and the legs, are tucked below. He is sitting on them. The grey mantle is pulled down and enlarged as he sits, but when he jumps up it shrinks somewhat, all his black-and-white marks are now shown, and just as his colours formerly whispered, 'I am a clod,' they now shout aloud, 'I am a Jack-rabbit.'

Why should he do this? Why should a timid creature running for his life thus proclaim to all the world his name instead of trying to hide? There must be some good reason. It must pay, or the Rabbit would never have done it. The answer is, if the creature that scared him up was one of his own kind – i.e., this was a false alarm – then at once, by showing his national colours, the mistake is made right. On the other hand, if it be a Coyote, Fox, or Dog, they see at once, this is a Jack-rabbit, and know that it would be waste of time for them to pursue him. They say in effect, 'This is a Jack-rabbit, and I cannot catch a Jack in open race.' They give it up, and that, of course, saves the Jack a great deal of unnecessary running and worry. The black-and-white spots are the national uniform and flag of the Jacks. In poor specimens they are apt to be dull, but in the finest specimens they are not only larger, but brighter than usual, and the Little Warhorse, grey when he sat in his form, blazed like charcoal and snow, when he flung his defiance to the Fox and buff Coyote, and danced with little effort before them, first a black-and-white Jack, then a little white spot, and last a speck of thistledown, before the distance swallowed him.

Many of the farmers' Dogs had learned the lesson: 'A

greyish Rabbit you may catch, but a very black-and-white one is hopeless.' They might, indeed, follow for a time, but that was merely for the fun of a chivvy, and his growing power often led Warhorse to seek the chase for the sake of a little excitement, and to take hazards that others less gifted were most careful to avoid.

Jack, like all other wild animals, had a certain range or country which was home to him, and outside of this he rarely strayed. It was about three miles across, extending easterly from the centre of the village. Scattered through this he had a number of 'forms', or 'beds' as they are locally called. These were mere hollows situated under a sheltering bush or bunch of grass, without lining excepting the accidental grass and in-blown leaves. But comfort was not forgotten. Some of them were for hot weather; they faced the north, were scarcely sunk, were little more than shady places. Some for the cold weather were deep hollows with southern exposure, and others for the wet were well roofed with herbage and faced the west. In one or other of these he spent the day, and at night he went forth to feed with his kind, sporting and romping on the moonlight nights like a lot of puppy Dogs, but careful to be gone by sunrise, and safely tucked in a bed that was suited to the weather.

The safest ground for the Jacks was among the farms, where not only Osage hedges, but also the newly arrived barb-wire, made hurdles and hazards in the path of possible enemies. But the finest of the forage is nearer to the village among the truck-farms – the finest of forage and the fiercest of dangers. Some of the dangers of the plains were lacking, but the greater perils of men, guns, Dogs, and impassable fences are much increased. Yet those who knew Warhorse best were not at all surprised to find that he had made a form in the middle of a market-gardener's melon-patch. A score of dangers beset him here, but there was also a score of unusual delights and a score of holes in the fence for times when he had to fly, with at least twoscore of expedients to help him afterwards.

III

Newchusen was a typical Western town. Everywhere in it, were to be seen strenuous efforts at uglification, crowned with unmeasured success. The streets were straight level lanes without curves or beauty-spots. The houses were cheap and mean structures of flimsy boards and tar paper, and not even honest in their ugliness, for each of them was pretending to be something better than itself. One had a false front to make it look like two storeys, another was of imitation brick, a third pretended to be a marble temple.

But all agreed in being the ugliest things ever used as human dwellings, and in each could be read the owner's secret thought – to stand it for a year or so, then move out somewhere else. The only beauties of the place, and those unintentional, were the long lines of hand-planted shade-trees, uglified as far as possible with whitewashed trunks and croppy heads, but still lovable, growing, living things.

The only building in town with a touch of picturesqueness was the grain elevator. It was not posing as a Greek temple or a Swiss chalet, but simply a strong, rough, honest, grain elevator. At the end of each street was a vista of the prairie, with its farm-houses, windmill pumps, and long lines of Osage-orange hedges. Here at least was something of interest – the grey-green hedges, thick, sturdy, and high, were dotted with their golden mock-oranges, useless fruit, but more welcome here than rain in a desert; for these balls were things of beauty, and swung on their long tough boughs they formed with the soft green leaves a colour-chord that pleased the weary eye.

Such a town is a place to get out of, as soon as possible, so thought the traveller who found himself laid over here for two days in late winter. He asked after the sights of the place. A white Muskrat stuffed in a case 'down to the saloon'; old Baccy Bullin, who had been scalped by the Indians forty years ago; and a pipe once smoked by Kit Carson, proved unattractive, so he turned towards the prairie, still white with snow.

A mark among the numerous Dog tracks caught his eye: it was the track of a large Jack-rabbit. He asked a passer-by if there were any Rabbits in town.

'No, I reckon not. I never seen none,' was the answer. A mill-hand gave the same reply, but a small boy with a bundle of newspapers said: 'You bet there is; there's lots of them out there on the prairie, and they come in town a-plenty. Why, there's a big, big feller lives right round Si Kalb's melon-patch – oh, an awful big feller, and just as black and as white as checkers!' and thus he sent the stranger eastward on his walk.

The 'big, big, awful big one' was the Little Warhorse himself. He didn't live in Kalb's melon-patch; he was there only at odd times. He was not there now; he was in his west-fronting form or bed, because a raw east wind was setting in. It was due east of Madison Avenue, and as the stranger plodded that way the Rabbit watched him. As long as the man kept the road the Jack was quiet, but the road turned shortly to the north, and the man by chance left it and came straight on. Then the Jack saw trouble ahead. The moment the man left the beaten track, he bounded from his form, and wheeling, he sailed across the prairie due east.

A Jack-rabbit running from its enemy ordinarily covers eight or nine feet at a bound, and once in five or six bounds, it makes an observation hop, leaping not along, but high in the air, so as to get above all herbage and bushes and take in the situation. A silly young Jack will make an observation hop as often as one in four, and so waste a great deal of time. A clever Jack will make one hop in eight or nine, do for observation. But Jack Warhorse as he sped, got all the information he needed, in one hop out of a dozen, while ten to fourteen feet were covered by each of his flying bounds. Yet another personal peculiarity showed in the trail he left. When a Cottontail or a Woodhare runs, his tail is curled up tight on his back, and does not touch the snow. When a Jack runs, his tail hangs downward or backward, with the tip curved or straight, according to the individual; in some, it points straight down, and so, often leaves a little stroke behind the foot-marks. The Warhorse's tail of shining black, was of unusual length, and at every bound, it left in the snow, a long stroke, so long that that alone was almost enough to tell which Rabbit had made the track.

Now some Rabbits seeing only a man without any Dog would have felt little fear, but Warhorse, remembering some former stinging experiences with a far-killer, fled when the foe was seventy-five yards away, and skimming low, he ran southeast to a fence that ran easterly. Behind this he went like a low-flying Hawk, till a mile away he reached another of his beds; and here, after an observation taken as he stood on his heels, he settled again to rest.

But not for long. In twenty minutes his great megaphone ears, so close to the ground, caught a regular sound – crunch, crunch, crunch – the tramp of a human foot, and he started up to see the man with the shining stick in his hand, now drawing near.

Warhorse bounded out and away for the fence. Never once did he rise to a 'spy-hop' till the wire and rails were between him and his foe, an unnecessary precaution as it chanced, for the man was watching the trail and saw nothing of the Rabbit.

Jack skimmed along, keeping low and looking out for other enemies. He knew now that the man was on his track, and the old instinct born of ancestral trouble with Weasels was doubtless what prompted him to do the double trail. He ran in a long, straight course to a distant fence, followed its far side for fifty yards, then doubling back he retraced his trail and ran off in a new direction till he reached another of his dens or forms. He had been out all night and was very ready to rest, now that the sun was ablaze on the snow; but he had hardly got the place a little warmed when the 'tramp, tramp, tramp' announced the enemy, and he hurried away.

After a half-a-mile run he stopped on a slight rise and marked the man still following, so he made a series of wonderful quirks in his trail, a succession of blind zigzags that would have puzzled most trailers; then running a hundred yards past a favourite form, he returned to it from the other side, and settled to rest, sure that now the enemy would be finally thrown off the scent.

It was slower than before, but still it came – 'tramp, tramp, tramp'.

Jack awoke, but sat still. The man tramped by on the trail one hundred yards in front of him, and as he went on, Jack sprang out unseen, realizing that this was an unusual occasion needing a special effort. They had gone in a vast circle around the home range of the Warhorse and now were less than a mile from the farm-house of the black Dog. There was that wonderful board fence with the happily planned hen-hole. It was a place of good memory – here more than once he had won, here specially he had baffled the Greyhound.

These doubtless were the motive thoughts rather than

any plan of playing one enemy against another, and Warhorse bounded openly across the snow to the fence of the big black Dog.

The hen-hole was shut, and Warhorse, not a little puzzled, sneaked around to find another, without success, until, around the front, here was the gate wide open, and inside lying on some boards was the big Dog, fast asleep. The Hens were sitting hunched up in the warmest corner of the yard. The house Cat was gingerly picking her way from barn to kitchen, as Warhorse halted in the gateway.

The black form of his pursuer was crawling down the far white prairie slope. Jack hopped quietly into the yard. A long-legged Rooster, that ought to have minded his own business, uttered a loud cackle as he saw the Rabbit hopping near. The Dog lying in the sun raised his head and stood up, and Jack's peril was dire. He squatted low and turned himself into a grey clod. He did it cleverly, but still might have been lost but for the Cat. Unwittingly, unwillingly, she saved him. The black Dog had taken three steps towards the Warhorse, though he did not know the Rabbit was there, and was now blocking the only way of escape from the yard, when the Cat came round the corner of the house, and leaping to a window-ledge brought a flower-pot rolling down. By that single awkward act she disturbed the armed neutrality existing between herself and the Dog. She fled to the barn, and of course a flying foe is all that is needed to send a Dog on the war-path. They passed within thirty feet of the crouching Rabbit. As soon as they were well gone, Jack turned, and without even a 'Thank you, Pussy', he fled to the open and away on the hard-beaten road.

The Cat had been rescued by the lady of the house; the Dog was once more sprawling on the boards when the man on Jack's trail arrived. He carried, not a gun, but a stout stick, sometimes called 'dog-medicine', and that was all that prevented the Dog attacking the enemy of his prey.

This seemed to be the end of the trail. The trick, whether planned or not, was a success, and the Rabbit got rid of his troublesome follower.

Next day the stranger made another search for the Jack and found, not himself, but his track. He knew it by its tail-mark, its long leaps and few spy-hops, but with it and running by it was the track of a smaller Rabbit. Here is where they met, here they chased each other in play, for no signs of battle were there to be seen; here they fed or sat together in the sun, there they ambled side by side, and here again they sported in the snow, always together. There was only one conclusion: this was the mating season. This was a pair of Jack-rabbits – the Little Warhorse and his mate.

IV

Next summer was a wonderful year for the Jack-rabbits. A foolish law had set a bounty on Hawks and Owls and had caused a general massacre of these feathered policemen. Consequently the Rabbits had multiplied in such numbers that they now were threatening to devastate the country.

The farmers, who were the sufferers from the bounty law, as well as the makers of it, decided on a great Rabbit drive. All the county was invited to come, on a given morning, to the main road north of the county, with the intention of sweeping the whole region up-wind and at length driving the Rabbits into a huge corral of close wire netting. Dogs were barred as unmanageable, and guns as dangerous in a crowd; but every man and boy carried a couple of long sticks and a bag full of stones. Women came on horseback and in buggies; many carried rattles or horns and tins to make a noise. A number of the buggies trailed a string of old cans or tied laths to scrape on the wheel-spokes, and thus add no little to the deafening clatter of the drive. As Rabbits have marvellously sensitive hearing, a noise that is distracting to mankind, is likely to prove bewildering to them.

The weather was right, and at eight in the morning the word to advance was given. The line was about five miles long at first, and there was a man or a boy every thirty or forty yards. The buggies and riders kept perforce almost entirely to the roads; but the beaters were supposed, as a point of honour, to face everything, and keep the front unbroken. The advance was roughly in three sides of a square. Each man made as much noise as he could, and threshed every bush in his path. A number of Rabbits hopped out. Some made for the lines, to be at once assailed by a shower of stones that laid many of them low. One or two did get through and escaped, but the majority were swept before the drive. At first the number seen was small, but before three miles were covered the Rabbits were running ahead in every direction. After five miles – and that took about three hours – the word for the wings to close in was given. The space between the men was shortened up till they were less than ten feet apart, and the whole drive converged on the corral with its two long guide wings or fences; the end lines joined these wings, and the surround was complete. The drivers marched rapidly now; scores of the Rabbits were killed as they ran too near the beaters. Their bodies strewed the ground, but the swarms seemed to increase; and in the final move, before the victims were cooped up in the corral, the two-acre space surrounded was a whirling throng of scurrying, jumping, bounding Rabbits. Round and round they circled and leaped, looking for a chance to escape; but the inexorable crowd grew thicker as the ring grew steadily smaller, and the whole swarm was forced along the chute into the tight corral, some to squat stupidly in the middle, some to race round the outer wall, some to seek hiding in corners or under each other.

And the Little Warhorse – where was he in all this? The drive had swept him along, and he had been one of the first to enter the corral. But a curious plan of selection had been established. The pen was to be a death-trap for the Rabbits, except the best, the soundest. And many were there that were unsound; those that think of all wild animals as pure and perfect things, would have been shocked to see how many halt, maimed, and diseased there were in that pen of four thousand or five thousand Jack-rabbits.

It was a Roman victory – the rabble of prisoners was to be butchered. The choicest were to be reserved for the arena. The arena? Yes, that is the Coursing Park.

In that corral trap, prepared beforehand for the Rabbits, were a number of small boxes along the wall, a whole series of them, five hundred at least, each large enough to hold one Jack.

In the last rush of driving, the swiftest Jacks got first to the pen. Some were swift and silly; when once inside they rushed wildly round and round. Some were swift and wise; they quickly sought the hiding afforded by the little boxes; all of these were now full. Thus five hundred of the swiftest and wisest had been selected, in, not by any means an infallible way, but the simplest and readiest. These five hundred were destined to be coursed by Greyhounds. The surging mass of over four thousand were ruthlessly given to slaughter.

Five hundred little boxes with five hundred bright-eyed Jack-rabbits were put on the train that day, and among them was Little Jack Warhorse.

V

Rabbits take their troubles lightly, and it is not to be supposed that any great terror was felt by the boxed Jacks, once the uproar of the massacre was over; and when they reached the Coursing Park near the great city and were turned out one by one, very gently – yes, gently; the Roman guards were careful of their prisoners, being responsible for them – the Jacks found little to complain of, a big enclosure with plenty of good food, and no enemies to annoy them.

The very next morning their training began. A score of hatchways were opened into a much larger field – the Park. After a number of Jacks had wandered out through these doors a rabble of boys appeared and drove them back, pursuing them noisily until all were again in the smaller field, called the Haven. A few days of this taught the Jack-rabbits that when pursued their safety was to get back by one of the hatches into the Haven.

Now the second lesson began. The whole band were driven out of a side door into a long lane which led around three sides of the Park to another enclosure at the far end. This was the Starting Pen. Its door into the arena – that is, the Park – was opened, the Rabbits driven forth, and then a mob of boys and Dogs in hiding, burst forth and pursued them across the open. The whole army went bobbing and bounding away, some of the younger ones soaring in a spy-hop, as a matter of habit; but low skimming ahead of them all was a gorgeous black-and-white one; clean-limbed and bright-eyed, he had attracted attention in the pen, but now in the field he led the band with easy lope that put him as far ahead of them all as they were ahead of the rabble of common Dogs.

'Luk at thot, would ye – but ain't he a Little Warhorse?' shouted a villainous-looking Irish stable-boy, and thus he was named. When halfway across the course the Jacks remembered the Haven, and all swept towards it and in like a snow-cloud over the drifts.

This was the second lesson – to lead straight for the Haven as soon as driven from the Pen. In a week all had learned it, and were ready for the great opening meet of the Coursing Club.

The Little Warhorse was now well known to the grooms and hangers-on; his colours usually marked him clearly, and his leadership was in a measure recognized by the long-eared herd that fled with him. He figured more or less with the Dogs in the talk and betting of the men.

'Wonder if old Dignam is going to enter Minkie this year?'

'Faix, an' if he does I bet the Little Warrhorrse will take the gimp out av her an' her runnin' mate.'

'I'll bet three to one that my old Jen will pick the Warhorse up before he passes the grand stand,' growled a dog-man.

'An' it's meself will take thot bet in dollars,' said Mickey, 'an', moore than thot, Oi'll put up a hull month's stuff thot there ain't a dog in the mate thot kin turrn the Warrhorrse oncet on the hull coorse.'

So they wrangled and wagered, but each day, as they put the Rabbits through their paces, there were more of those who believed that they had found a wonderful runner in the Warhorse, one that would give the best Greyhounds something that is rarely seen, a straight stern chase from Start to Grand Stand and Haven.

VI

The first morning of the meet arrived bright and promising. The Grand Stand was filled with a city crowd. The usual types of a racecourse appeared in force. Here and there were to be seen the dog-grooms leading in leash single Greyhounds or couples, shrouded in blankets, but showing their sinewy legs, their snaky necks, their shapely heads with long reptilian jaws, and their quick, nervous yellow eyes – hybrids of natural force and human ingenuity, the most wonderful running-machines ever made of flesh and blood. Their keepers guarded them like jewels, tended them like babies, and were careful to keep them from picking up odd eatables, as well as prevent them smelling unusual objects or being approached by strangers. Large sums were wagered on these Dogs, and a cunningly placed tack, a piece of doctored meat, yes, an artfully compounded smell, has been known to turn a superb young runner into a lifeless laggard, and to the owner this might spell *ruin*. The Dogs entered in each class are paired off, as each contest is supposed to be a duel; the winners in the first series are then paired again. In each trial, a Jack is driven from the Starting-pen; close by in one leash are the rival Dogs, held by the slipper. As soon as the Hare is well away, the man has to get the Dogs evenly started and slip them together. On the field is the judge, scarlet-coated and well mounted. He follows the chase. The Hare, mindful of his training, speeds across the open, towards the Haven, in full view of the Grand Stand. The Dogs follow the Jack. As the first one comes near enough to be dangerous, the Hare balks him by dodging. Each time the Hare is turned, scores for the Dog that did it, and a final point is made by the kill.

Sometimes the kill takes place within one hundred yards of the start – that means a poor Jack; mostly it happens in front of the Grand Stand; but on rare occasions it chances that the Jack goes sailing across the open Park a good half-mile and, by dodging for time, runs to safety in the Haven. Four finishes are possible: a speedy kill; a speedy winning of the Haven; new Dogs to relieve the first runners, who would suffer heart-collapse in the terrific strain of their pace, if kept up many minutes in hot weather; and finally, for Rabbits that by continued dodging defy and jeopardize the Dogs, and yet do not win the Haven, there is kept a *loaded shotgun*.

There is just as much jockeying at a Kaskado coursing as at a Kaskado horse-race, just as many attempts at fraud, and it is just as necessary to have the judge and slipper beyond suspicion.

The day before the next meet a man of diamonds saw Irish Mickey – by chance. A cigar was all that visibly passed, but it had a green wrapper that was slipped off before lighting. Then a word: 'If you wuz slipper tomorrow and it so came about that Dignam's Minkie gets done, wall – it means another cigar.'

'Faix, an' if I wuz slipper I could load the dice so Minkie would niver score a p'int, but her runnin' mate would have the same bad luck.'

'That so?' The diamond man looked interested. 'All right – fix it so; it means two cigars.'

Slipper Slyman had always dealt on the square, had scorned many approaches – that was well known. Most believed in him, but there were some malcontents, and when a man with many gold seals approached the Steward and formulated charges, serious and well-backed, they must perforce suspend the slipper pending an enquiry, and thus Mickey Doo reigned in his stead.

Mickey was poor and not over-scrupulous. Here was a chance to make a year's pay in a minute, nothing wrong about it, no harm to the Dog or the Rabbit either.

One Jack-rabbit is much like another. Everybody knows that; it was simply a question of choosing your Jack.

The preliminaries were over. Fifty Jacks had been run and killed. Mickey had done his work satisfactorily; a fair slip had been given to every leash. He was still in command as slipper. Now came the final for the cup – the cup and the large stakes.

VII

There were the slim and elegant Dogs awaiting their turn. Minkie and her rival were first. Everything had been fair so far, and who can say that what followed was unfair? Mickey could turn out which Jack he pleased.

'Number three!' he called to his partner.

Out leaped the Little Warhorse – black and white his great ears, easy and low his five-foot bounds; gazing wildly at the unwonted crowd about the Park, he leaped high in one surprising spy-hop.

'Hrrrrr!' shouted the slipper, and his partner rattled a stick on the fence. The Warhorse's bounds increased to eight or nine feet.

'Hrrrrrr!' and they were ten or twelve feet. At thirty yards the Hounds were slipped – an even slip; some thought it could have been done at twenty yards.

'Hrrrrrr! Hrrrrrrr!' and the Warhorse was doing fourteen-foot leaps, not a spy-hop among them.

'Hrrrrr!' wonderful Dogs! how they sailed; but drifting ahead of them, like a white seabird or flying scud, was the Warhorse. Away past the Grand Stand. And the Dogs –

were they closing the gap of start? Closing! It was lengthening! In less time than it takes to tell it, the black-and-white thistledown had drifted away through the Haven door – the door so like that good old hen-hole – and the Greyhounds pulled up amidst a roar of derision and cheers for the Little Warhorse. How Mickey did laugh! How Dignam did swear! How the newspaper men did scribble – scribble – scribble!

Next day there was a paragraph in all the papers: 'WONDERFUL FEAT OF A JACK-RABBIT. The Little Warhorse, as he has been styled, completely skunked two of the most famous Dogs on the turf,' etc.

There was a fierce wrangle among the dog-men. This was a tie, since neither had scored, and Minkie and her rival were allowed to run again; but that half-mile had been too hot, and they had no show for the cup.

Mickey met 'Diamonds' next day, *by chance.*

'Have a cigar, Mickey.'

'Oi will thot, sor. Faix, thim's so foine, I'd loike two – thank ye, sor.'

VIII

From that time the Little Warhorse became the pride of the Irish boy. Slipper Slyman had been honourably reinstated and Mickey reduced to the rank of Jack-starter, but that merely helped to turn his sympathies from the Dogs to the Rabbits, or rather to the Warhorse, for of all the five hundred that were brought in from the drive he alone had won renown. There were several that crossed the Park to run again another day, but he alone had crossed the course without getting even a turn. Twice a week the meets took place; forty or fifty Jacks were killed each time, and the five hundred in the pen had been nearly all eaten of the arena.

The Warhorse had run each day, and as often had made the Haven. Mickey became wildly enthusiastic about his favourite's powers. He begot a positive affection for the clean-limbed racer, and stoutly maintained against all that it was a positive honour to a Dog to be disgraced by such a Jack.

It is so seldom that a Rabbit crosses the track at all, that when Jack did it six times without having to dodge, the papers took note of it, and after each meet there appeared a notice: 'The Little Warhorse crossed again today; old-timers say it shows how our Dogs are deteriorating.'

After the sixth time the rabbit-keepers grew enthusiastic, and Mickey, commander-in-chief of the brigade, became intemperate in his admiration. 'Be jabers, he has a right to be torned loose. He has won his freedom loike ivery Amerikin done,' he added, by way of appeal to the patriotism of the Steward of the race, who was, of course, the real owner of the Jacks.

'All right, Mick; if he gets across thirteen times you can ship him back to his native land,' was the reply.

'Shure now, an' won't you make it tin, sor?'

'No, no; I need him to take the conceit out of some of the new Dogs that are coming.'

'Thirteen toimes and he is free, sor; it's a bargain.'

A new lot of Rabbits arrived about this time, and one of these was coloured much like Little Warhorse. He had no such speed, but to prevent mistakes Mickey caught his favourite by driving him into one of the padded shipping-boxes, and proceeded with the gate-keeper's punch to ear-mark him. The punch was sharp; a clear star was cut out of the thin flap, when Mickey exclaimed: 'Faix, an' Oi'll punch for ivery toime ye cross the coorse.' So he cut six stars in a row. 'Thayer now, Warrhorrse, shure it's a free Rabbit ye'll be when ye have yer thirteen stars loike our flag of liberty hed when *we* got free.'

Within a week the Warhorse had vanquished the new Greyhounds and had stars enough to go round the right ear and begin on the left. In a week more the thirteen runs were completed, six stars in the left ear and seven in the right, and the newspapers had new material.

'Whoop!' How Mickey hoorayed! 'An' it's a free Jack ye are, Warrhorrse! Thirteen always wuz a lucky number. I never knowed it to fail.'

IX

'Yes, I know I did,' said the Steward. 'But I want to give him one more run. I have a bet on him against a new Dog here. It won't hurt him now; he can do it. Oh, well. Here now, Mickey, don't you get sassy. One run more this afternoon. The Dogs run two or three times a day; why not the Jack?'

'They're not shtakin' thayre loives, sor.'

'Oh, you get out.'

Many more Rabbits had been added to the pen – big and small, peaceful and warlike – and one big Buck of savage instincts, seeing Jack Warhorse's hurried dash into the Haven that morning, took advantage of the moment to attack him.

At another time Jack would have thumped his skull, as he once did the Cat's, and settled the affair in a minute; but now it took several minutes, during which he himself got roughly handled; so when the afternoon came he was suffering from one or two bruises and stiffening wounds; not serious, indeed, but enough to lower his speed.

The start was much like those of previous runs. The Warhorse steaming away low and lightly, his ears up and the breezes whistling through his thirteen stars.

Minkie with Fango, the new Dog, bounded in eager pursuit, but, to the surprise of the starters, the gap grew smaller. The Warhorse was losing ground, and right before the Grand Stand old Minkie turned him, and a cheer went up from the dog-men, for all knew the runners. Within fifty yards Fango scored a turn, and the race was right back to the start. There stood Slyman and Mickey. The Rabbit dodged, the Greyhounds plunged; Jack could not get away, and just as the final snap seemed near, the Warhorse leaped straight for Mickey, and in an instant was hidden in his arms, while the starter's feet flew out in energetic kicks to repel the furious Dogs. It is not likely that the Jack knew Mickey for a friend; he only yielded to the old instinct to fly from a certain enemy to a neutral or a possible friend, and, as luck would have it, he had wisely leaped and well. A cheer went up from the benches as Mickey hurried back with his favourite. But the dog-men protested 'it wasn't a fair run – they wanted it finished'. They appealed to the Steward. He had backed the Jack against Fango. He was sore now, and ordered a new race.

An hour's rest was the best Mickey could get for him. Then he went as before, with Fango and Minkie in pursuit. He seemed less stiff now – he ran more like himself; but a little past the Stand he was turned by Fango and again by Minkie, and back and across, and here and there, leaping frantically and barely eluding his foes. For several minutes it lasted. Mickey could see that Jack's ears were sinking. The new Dog leaped. Jack dodged almost under him to escape, and back only to meet the second Dog; and now both ears were flat on his back. But the Hounds were suffering too. Their tongues were lolling out; their jaws and heaving sides were splashed with foam. The Warhorse's ears went up again. His courage seemed to revive in their distress. He made a straight dash for the Haven; but the straight dash was just what the Hounds could do, and within a hundred yards he was turned again, to begin another desperate game of zigzag. Then the dog-men saw danger for their Dogs, and two new ones were slipped – two fresh Hounds; surely they could end the race. *But they did not*. The first two were vanquished – gasping – out of it, but the next two were racing near. The Warhorse put forth all his strength. He left the first two far behind – was nearly to the Haven when the second two came up.

Nothing but dodging could save him now. His ears were sinking, his heart was pattering on his ribs, but his spirit was strong. He flung himself in wildest zigzags. The Hounds tumbled over each other. Again and again they thought they had him. One of them snapped off the end of his long black tail, yet he escaped; but he could not get to the Haven. The luck was against him. He was forced nearer to the Grand Stand. A thousand ladies were watching. The time limit was up. The second Dogs were suffering, when Mickey came running, yelling like a madman – words – imprecations – crazy sounds:

'Ye blackguard hoodlums! Ye dhirty, cowardly bastes!' and he rushed furiously at the Dogs, intent to do them bodily harm.

Officers came running and shouting, and Mickey, shrieking hatred and defiance, was dragged from the field, reviling Dogs and men with every horrid, insulting name he could think of or invent.

'Fair play! Whayer's yer fair play, ye liars, ye dhirty cheats, ye bloody cowards!' And they drove him from the arena. The last he saw of it was the four foaming Dogs feebly dodging after a weak and worn-out Jack-rabbit, and the judge on his Horse beckoning to the man with the gun.

The gate closed behind him, and Mickey heard a *bang – bang*, an unusual uproar mixed with yelps of Dogs, and he knew that Little Jack Warhorse had been served with finish No. 4.

All his life he had loved Dogs, but his sense of fair play was outraged. He could not get in, nor see in from where he was. He raced along the lane to the Haven, where he might get a good view, and arrived in time to see – Little Jack Warhorse with his half-masted ears limp into the Haven; and he realized at once that the man with the gun had missed, had hit the wrong runner, for there was the crowd at the Stand watching two men who were carrying a wounded Greyhound, while a veterinary surgeon was ministering to another that was panting on the ground.

Mickey looked about, seized a little shipping-box, put it at the angle of the Haven, carefully drove the tired thing into it, closed the lid, then, with the box under his arm, he scaled the fence unseen in the confusion and was gone.

'It didn't matter; he had lost his job anyway.' He tramped away from the city. He took the train at the nearest station and travelled some hours, and now he was in Rabbit country again. The sun had long gone down; the night with its stars was over the plain when among the farms, the Osage and alfalfa, Mickey Doo opened the box and gently put the Warhorse out.

Grinning as he did so, he said: 'Shure an' it's ould Oireland thot's proud to set the thirteen stars at liberty wance moore.'

For a moment the Little Warhorse gazed in doubt, then took three or four long leaps and a spy-hop to get his bearings. Now spreading his national colours and his honour-marked ears, he bounded into his hard-won freedom, strong as ever, and melted into the night of his native plain.

He has been seen many times in Kaskado, and there have been many Rabbit drives in that region, but he seems to know some means of baffling them now, for, in all the thousands that have been trapped and corralled, they have never since seen the star-spangled ears of Little Jack War-horse.

A Street Troubadour

Being the Adventures of a Cock Sparrow

I

Such a chirruping, such a twittering, and such a squirming, fluttering mass! Half a dozen English Sparrows rolling over and chattering around one another in the Fifth Avenue gutter, and in the middle of the mob, when it scattered somewhat, could be seen the cause of it all – a little Hen Sparrow, vigorously, indignantly defending herself against her crowd of noisy suitors. They seemed to be making love to her, but their methods were so rough they might have been a lynching party. They plucked, worried, and harried the indignant little lady in a manner utterly disgraceful, except that it was noticeable they did her no serious harm. She, however, laid about her with a will. Under no compulsion to spare her tormentors, apparently she would have slaughtered them all if she could.

It seemed clear that they were making love to her, but it seemed equally clear that she wanted none of them, and having partly convinced them of this at the point of her beak, she took advantage of a brief scattering of the assailants to fly up to the nearest eaves, displaying in one wing, as she went, some white feathers that afforded a mark to know her by, and may have been one of her chief charms.

II

A Cock Sparrow, in the pride of his black cravat and white collar-points, was hard at work building in a bird-house that some children had set on a pole in the garden for such as he. He was a singular Bird in several respects. The building-material that he selected was all twigs, that must have been brought from Madison or Union Square, and in the early morning he sometimes stopped work for a minute to utter a loud sweet song, much like that of a Canary.

It is not usual for a Cock Sparrow to build alone. But then this was an unusual Bird. After a week he had apparently finished the nest, for the bird-house was crammed to the very door with twigs purloined from the municipal shade-trees. He had now more leisure for music, and astonished the people about by frequent rendering of his long, unsparrow-like ditty; and he might have gone down to history as an unaccountable mystery, but that a barber bird-fancier on Sixth Avenue supplied the missing chapters of his early life.

This man, it seems, had put a Sparrow's egg into the wicker basket-nest of his Canaries. The youngster had duly hatched, and had been trained by the foster-parents. Their specialty was song. He had the lungs and robustness of his own race. The Canaries had trained him well, and the result was a songster who made up in energy what he lacked in native talent. Strong and pugnacious, as well as musical, this vociferous roustabout had soon made himself master of the cage. He had no hesitation in hammering into silence a Canary that he could not put down by musical superiority, and after one of these little victories his strains were so unusually good that the barber had a stuffed Canary provided for the boisterous musician to vanquish whenever he wished to favour some visitor with Randy's exultant paeans of victory. He worried into silent subjection all of the Canaries he was caged with, and when finally kept by himself nothing angered him more than to be near some voluble songster that he could neither silence nor get at. On these occasions he forgot his music, and his own Sparrow nature showed in the harsh *chirrup*, *chirrup* that has apparently been developed to make itself appreciated in the din of street traffic.

By the time his black bib had appeared he had made himself one of the chief characters and quite the chief attraction of the barber-shop. But one day the shelf on which the bird-cages stood gave way, all the cages were dashed to the floor, and in the general smash many of the Birds escaped. Among them was Randy, or, more properly, Bertrand, as this pugnacious songster was named after the famous Troubadour. The Canaries had voluntarily returned to their cages, or permitted themselves to be caught. But Randy hopped out of a back window, chirruped a few times, sang a defiant answer to the elevated-railway whistle, and keeping just out of reach of all attempts to capture him, he began to explore the brick wilderness about. He had not been a prisoner for generations. He readily accepted the new condition of freedom, and within a week was almost as wild as any of his kin, and had degenerated into a little street rowdy like the others, squabbling among them in the gutter, giving them blow for blow, or surprising all hearers with occasional bursts of Canary music delivered with Sparrow energy.

III

This, then, was Randy, who had selected the bird-house for a nesting-place, and the reason for his intemperance in the matter of twigs is now clear. The only nest he had ever known was of basketwork; therefore a proper nest is made of twigs.

Within a few days Randy appeared with a mate. I might have forgotten the riot scene in the gutter, as such things are common, but that I now recognized in Randy's bride the little white-winged Biddy Sparrow that had caused it.

She had apparently accepted Randy, but she was still putting on airs, pecking at him when he came near. He was squirming around with drooping wings and tilted tail, chirping like any other ardent Cock Sparrow, but occasionally stopping to show off his Canary accomplishment.

Any objections she may have had were apparently overcome, possibly by this astonishing display of genius, and he escorted her to the ready-made nest, running in ahead to show the way, and hopping proudly, noisily, officiously about her. She followed him, but came out again quickly, with Randy after her chirping and beseeching. He chattered a long time before he could persuade her to re-enter, but again she came out immediately, this time sputtering and scolding. Again he seemed to exert his power of persuasion, and finally she went in chattering, reappeared with a twig in her bill, dropped it, and flew away out of sight. Randy came out. All his joy and pride in his house were gone. This was a staggering blow, when he had looked for unmitigated commendation. He sat disconsolately on the door-step for a minute, and chirruped in a way that probably meant, 'Come back, come back!' But his bride did not come. He turned into the house. There was a scratching sound, and he came out at once with a large stick and flung it from the door to the ground. He returned for another, sent that flying after the first, and so went on, dragging out and hurling down all the sticks he had so carefully and laboriously carried in. That wonderful forked one that had given so much trouble to get here from Union Square, and those two smooth ones, just like the ones in his foster-mother's nest – all, all must go. For over an hour he toiled away in silence and alone. Then, apparently he had ended his task, for on the ground below was a pile of sticks, as big as a bonfire, the labour of a week undone. Randy glared fiercely at them and at the empty house, gave a short, harsh chirp, probably a Sparrow bad word, then flew away.

Next day he reappeared with Biddy, fussing about her in passerine exuberance once more, and chirping as he led her to the door again. She hopped in, then out, looked aslant at the twigs below, went back in, reappeared with a very small twig that had been overlooked, dropped it, and with evident satisfaction watched it fall on the pile below. After running in and out a dozen times they set off together, and presently returned, Biddy with her bill full of hay, Randy with one straw. These were carried in and presumably arranged satisfactorily. Then they went for more hay, and having got Randy set right, she remained in the box to arrange the hay as he brought it, only occasionally going for a load when he was long in coming. It was marvellous to see how the chivalry in this aggressive musician was reducing him to subjection. It seemed a good opportunity to try their tastes. I put out thirty short strings and ribbons in a row on a balcony near. Fifteen were common strips, eight were gaudy strips, and seven were bright silk ribbons. Every other one in the row was a dull string. Biddy was the first to see this array of material. She flew down, looked over it, around it, left eye, right eye; then decided to let it alone. But Randy came closer; he was not unfamiliar with threads. He hopped this way, then that, pulled at a thread, started back, but came nearer, nibbled at one or two, then made a dart at a string and bore it away. Next time Biddy came, and each bore off a string. They took only the dull ones, but after these were gone Biddy selected some of the brighter material, though even she did not venture on the gaudiest ribbons, and Randy would have no hand in bringing home any but the soberest and most stick-like materials. The nest was now half done. Randy once more ventured to carry in a stick, but a moment later it was whirling down to the pile below, with Biddy triumphantly gazing after it. Poor Randy! no toleration for *his* hobby – all those splendid sticks wasted. His mother had had a stick nest – a beautiful nest it was – but he was overruled. Nothing but straw now; then, not sticks, but softer material. He submitted – liberty had brought daily lessons of submission. He used to think that the barber-shop was the whole world and himself the most important living being. But of late both these ideas had been badly shaken. Biddy found that his education had been sadly neglected in all useful matters, and in each new kind of material she had to instruct him anew.

When the nest was two thirds finished, Biddy, whose ideas were quite luxurious, began to carry in large soft feathers. But now Randy thought this was going too far. He must draw the line somewhere. He drew it at feather beds. His earliest cradle had had no such lining. He proceeded to bundle out the objectionable feather bedding, and Biddy, returning with a new load, was just in time to see the first lot float downward from the door to join the stick pile below. She fluttered after them, seized them in the air, and returned to meet her lord coming out of the door with more of the obnoxious plumes, and there they stood, glaring at each other, chattering their loudest, their mouths full of feathers, and their hearts full of indignation.

How is it that when it is a question of home furnishing we sympathize with the female? I felt that Biddy had first right, and in the end she got her way. First there was a stormy time in which quantities of feathers were carried in and out of the house, or wind-borne about the garden. Then there was a lull, and next day all the feathers were carried back to the nest. Just how they arranged the matter will never be known, but it is sure that Randy himself did the greater part of the work, and never stopped till the box was crammed with the largest and softest of feathers. During all this they were usually together, but one day Biddy went off and stayed for some time. Randy looked about, chirruped, got no answer, looked up, then down, and far below he saw the pile of sticks that he had toiled to bring. Those dear sticks, just like the home of his early days! Randy fluttered down. There was the curious forked one still. The temptation was irresistible. Randy picked it up and hurried to the nest, then in. It had always been a difficult twig to manage – that side prong would catch at the door; but he had carried it so often now that he knew how. After half a minute's delay inside, while he was placing it, I suppose, he came out again, looked perkily about, preened and shook himself, then sang his Canary song from beginning to end several times, tried some new bars, and seemed extremely happy. When Biddy came with more feathers, he assiduously helped her to place them inside, and then the nest was finished. Two days later I got up to the nest, and in it found one egg. The Sparrows saw me go up, but did not fly chattering about my head, as do most Birds. They flew away to a distance, and watched anxiously from the shelter of some chimneys.

The third day there was a great commotion in the box,

a muffled scuffling and chattering, and once or twice a tail appeared at the door as though the owner were trying to back out. Then it seemed that something was being dragged about. At length the owner of the tail came out far enough to show that it was Biddy; but, apparently, she was pulled in again. Evidently a disgraceful family brawl was on. It was quite unaccountable, until finally Biddy struggled out of the door, dragging Randy's pet twig to throw it contemptuously on the ground below. She had discovered it in the bedding where he had hidden it; hence the row. But I do not see how she could drag it out when he was resisting. I suspect that he really weakened for the sake of peace. In the scuffle and general upset the egg – their first arrival – was unfortunately tumbled out with the stick, and fell down to lie below, in porcelain fragments, on a wet yellow background. The Sparrows did not seem to trouble about the remains. Having dropped from the nest, it had dropped out of their world.

IV

After this the pair got along peaceably for several days. Egg after egg was added to the nest. In a week there were five, and the two seemed now to be quite happy together. Randy sang to the astonishment of all the neighbourhood, and Biddy carried in more feathers as though preparing to set and anticipating a blizzard. But about this time it occurred to me to try a little experiment with the pair. Watching my chance, late one evening, I dropped a marble into the luxurious nest. What happened at once I do not know, but early the next morning I was out on Fifth Avenue near the corner of Twenty-first Street. It was Sunday. The street was very quiet, but a ring of perhaps a dozen people were standing gazing at something in the gutter. As I came near I heard occasional chirruping, and getting a view into the ring, I saw two Sparrows locked in fierce combat, chirruping a little, but hammering and pecking away in deadly earnest. They scuffled around, regardless of the bystanders, for some time; but when at length they paused for breath, and sat back on their tails and heels to gasp, I was quite shocked to recognize Biddy and Randy. After another round they were shooed away by one of the onlookers, who evidently disapproved of Sunday brawling. They then flew to the nearest roof to go on as before. That afternoon I found below the nest not only the intrusive marble, but also the remains of the five eggs, all alike thrown out, and I suspect that the presence of that curious hard round egg in the nest, and the obvious implication, were the cause of the brawl.

Whether Biddy had been able to explain it or not I do not know, but it seemed that the couple decided to forget the past and begin again. There was evidently neither luck nor peace in that bird-box, so they abandoned it, feathers and all; and Biddy, whose ideas were distinctly original, selected the site this time, nothing less than the top of an electric lamp in the middle of Madison Square. All week they laboured, and in spite of a high wind most of the time, they finished the nest. It is hard to see how the Birds could sleep at night with that great glaring buzzing light under their noses. Still, Biddy seemed pleased, Randy was learning to suppress his own opinion, and all would have gone well but that before the first egg was laid the carbon-points of the light burned out, and the man who put in the new ones thought proper to consign remorselessly the whole of the Biddy-Randy mansion to the garbage-can. A Robin or a Swallow might have felt this a crushing blow, but there is no limit to a Sparrow's energy and hopefulness. Evidently it was the wrong kind of a nest. Probably the material was at fault. At any rate, a radical change would be much better. After embezzling some long straws from the nest of an absent neighbour, Biddy laid them in the high fork of an elm-tree in Madison Square Park, by way of letting Randy know that this was the place now selected; and Randy, having learned by this time that it was less trouble to accept her decision than to offer an opinion of his own, sang a Canary trill on two chirps, and set about rummaging in the garbage-heaps for choice building-material, winking hard and looking the other way when a nice twig presented itself.

V

On the other side of the Square was the nest of a pair of very unpopular Sparrows. The male bird in particular had made himself thoroughly disliked. He was a big, handsome fellow with an enormous black cravat, but an out-and-out bully. Might is right in Sparrow world. Their causes for quarrel are food, mates, quarters, and nesting-material – pretty much as with ourselves. This arrogant little Bird, by reason of his strength, had the mate of his choice and the best nesting-site, and was adding to it all the most-admired material in the Square. My Sparrows had avoided the gaudy ribbons I offered. They were not educated up to that pitch, but they certainly had their aesthetic preferences. A few Guinea-fowl feathers that originally came from Central Park Menagerie had been stolen from one nest to another, till now they rested in the sumptuous home with which Cravat and his wife had embellished one of the marble capitals of the new bank. The Bully did much as he pleased in the Park, and one day, on hearing Randy's song, flew at him. Randy had been a terror among Canaries, but against

Cravat he had but little chance. He did his best, but was defeated, and took refuge in flight. Puffed up by this victory, the Bully flew to Randy's new nest, and after a more or less scornful scrutiny proceeded to drag out some strings that he thought he might use at home. Randy had been worsted, but the sight of this pillage roused the doughty Troubadour again, and he flew at the Bully as before. From the branches they tumbled to the ground. Other Sparrows joined in, and, shame to tell! they joined with the big fellow against the comparative stranger. Randy was getting very roughly handled, feathers began to float away, when into the ring flashed a little Hen Sparrow with white wing-feathers, chirrup, chirrup, wallop, wallop, she went into it. Oh, how she did lay about her! The Sparrows that had joined in for fun now went off: there was no longer any fun in it, nothing but hard pecks, and the tables were completely turned on Cravat. He quickly lost heart, then, and fled towards his own quarter of the Square, with Biddy holding on to his tail like a little bulldog; and there she continued to hang till the feather came out by the roots, and she afterwards had the satisfaction of working it into the coarser make-up of her nest along with the rescued material. It is hardly possible that Sparrows have refined ideas of justice and retribution, but it is sure that things which look like it do crop up among them. Within two days the Guinea-fowl feathers that had so long been the chief glory of the Cravat's nest now formed part of the furnishing of Biddy's new abode, and none had the temerity to dispute her claim.

It was now late in the season, feathers were scarce, and Biddy could not find enough for the lining that she was so particular about. But she found a substitute that appealed to her love of the novel. In the Square was the cab-stand, and scattering near were usually more or less horsehairs.

These seemed to be good and original linings. A most happy thought, and with appropriate enthusiasm the ever-hopeful couple set about gathering horsehairs, two or three at a time. Possibly the nest of a Chipping Sparrow in one of the parks gave them the idea. The Chippy always lines with horsehair, and gets an admirable spring-mattress effect by curling the hair round and round the inside of the nest. The result is good, but one must know how to get it. It would have been well had the Sparrows learned how to handle the hair. When a Chippy picks up a horsehair to bring home it takes only one at a time, and is careful to lift it by the end, for the harmless-looking hair is not without its dangers. The Sparrows had no notion of handling it except as they did the straw. Biddy seized a hair near the middle, found it somewhat long, so took a second hold, several inches away. In most cases this made a great loop in the hair over her head or beyond her beak. But it was a convenient way to manage, and at first no mischief came, though Chippy, had she seen, might well have shuddered at the idea of that threatening noose.

It was the last day of the lining. Biddy had in some way given Randy to understand that no more hair was needed, and, proud and bustling, she was adding a few finishing touches and a final hair while he was trying some new variations of his finest bars on top of Farragut's head, when a loud alarm chirrup from Biddy caught his ear. He looked towards the new home to see her struggling up and down without apparent reason, and yet unable to get more than her length away from the nest. She had at last put her head through one of those dangerous hair nooses, made by herself, and by mischance had tightened and twisted it so that she was caught. The more she struggled and twisted the tighter became the noose. Randy now discovered that he was deeply attached to this wilful little termagant. He became greatly excited, and flew about chattering. He tried to release her by pulling at her foot, but that only made matters worse. All their efforts were in vain. Several new kinks were added to the hair. Other hairs from the nest seemed to join in the plot, and, tangled and intermeshed, they tightened even more, till the group of wondering, upturned child faces in the Park below were centred on a tousled feathery form hanging still and silent in the place of the bustling, noisy, energetic Biddy Sparrow.

Poor Randy seemed deeply distressed. The neighbour Sparrows had come at the danger-call note, and joined their cries with his, but had not been able to help the victim. Now they went off to their own squabbles and troubles, and Randy hopped about chirping or sat still with drooping wings. It was long before he realized that she was dead, and all that day he exerted himself to interest her and make her join in their usual life. At night he rested alone in one of the trees, and at grey dawn was bustling about, singing occasionally and chirruping around the nest, from whose rim, in the fateful horsehair, hung Biddy, stiff and silent now.

VI

Randy had never been an alert Sparrow. His Canary training had really handicapped him. He was venturesome and heedless with carriages as well as with children. This peculiarity was greatly increased by his present preoccupation, and while foraging somewhat listlessly on Madison Avenue, that afternoon, a messenger-boy on a wheel came silently up, and before Randy realized his danger, the wheel was on his tail. As he struggled to get away, even at the price of his tail, his right wing flashed under the hind wheel, and then he was crippled. The boy rode on, and Randy managed to flutter and hop away towards the sheltering trees. A little girl, assisted by her small dog, captured the cripple, after an exciting chase among the benches. She took him home, and moved by what her brothers considered sadly misplaced tenderness, she caged and nursed him. When he began to recover, he one day surprised them by singing his Canary song.

This created quite a stir in the household. In time a newspaper reporter heard of it. The inevitable write-up followed, and this met the eye of the Sixth Avenue barber. He came with many witnesses to claim his bird, and at length his claim was allowed.

So Randy is once more in a cage, carefully watched and fed, the central figure in a small world, and not at all unhappy. After all, he was never a truly wild Bird. It was an accident that set him free originally. An accident had mated him with Biddy. Their brief life together had been a succession of storms and accidents. An accident had taken her away, and another accident had renewed his cage life. This life, comparatively calm and uneventful, has given him an opportunity to cultivate his musical gifts, for he is in a very conservatory of music, and close at hand are his old tutors and foster-parents.

Sometimes when left alone he amuses himself by beginning a rude nest of sticks, but he looks guilty, and leaves that corner of the cage when any one comes near. If a few feathers are given him they are worked into the nest at first, but next morning are invariably found on the floor below. These persistent attempts at nesting suggested that he wanted a mate, and several were furnished on approval, but the result was not happy. Prompt interference was needed each time to prevent bloodshed and to rescue the intended bride. So the attempt was given up. Evidently this Troubadour wants no new lady-love. His songs seem to be rather of war, for the barber has discovered that when he wishes to provoke Randy into his most rapturous musical expression it is only necessary to let him demolish, not the effigy of a Canary, but a stuffed Cocked Sparrow. And on these occasions Randy develops an enthusiasm almost amounting to inspiration if the dummy have a very well marked black patch on the throat.

This, however, is mere by-play. All his best energies are devoted to song. And if you stumble on the right barber-shop you may see this energetic recluse, forgetting the cares, joys, and sorrows of active life in his devotion to music, like some monk who has tried the world, found it too hard for him, and has gladly returned to his cell, there to devote the rest of his days to purely spiritual pleasures.

The Kangaroo Rat

I

It was a rough, rock-built, squalid ranch-house that I lived in, on the Currumpaw. The plaster of the walls was mud, the roof and walls were dry mud, the great river-flat around it was sandy mud, and the hills a mile away were piled-up mud, sculptured by frost and rain into the oddest of mud vagaries, with here and there a coping of lava to prevent the utter demolition of some necessary mud pinnacle by the indefatigable sculptors named.

The place seemed uninviting to a stranger from the lush and fertile prairies of Manitoba, but the more I saw of it the more it was revealed a paradise. For every cottonwood of the straggling belt that the river used to mark its doubtful course across the plain, and every dwarfed and spiny bush and weedy copse, was teeming with *life*. And every day and every night I made new friends, or learned new facts about the mudland denizens.

Man and the Birds are understood to possess the earth during the daylight, therefore the night has become the time for the four-footed ones to be about, and in order that

I might set a sleepless watch on their movements I was careful each night before going to bed to sweep smooth the dust about the shanty and along the two pathways, one to the spring and one to the corral by way of the former corn-patch, still called the 'garden'.

Each morning I went out with all the feelings of a child meeting the Christmas postman, or a fisherman hauling in his largest net, eager to know what there was for me.

Not a morning passed without a message from the beasts. Nearly every night a Skunk or two would come and gather up table-scraps, prying into all sorts of forbidden places in their search. Once or twice a Bobcat came. And one morning the faithful dust reported in great detail how the Bobcat and the Skunk had differed. There was evidence, too, that the Bobcat quickly said (in Bobcat, of course), 'I beg pardon, I mistook you for a rabbit, but will never again make such a mistake.'

More than once the sinister trail of the 'Hydrophoby-cat' was recorded. And on one occasion the great broad track of the King Wolf of the region came right up the pathway, nearly to the door, the tracks getting closer together as he neared it. Then stopping, he had exactly retraced his steps and gone elsewhere about his business. Jack-rabbits, Coyotes, and Cottontails all passed, and wrote for me a few original lines commemorative of their visit – and all were faithfully delivered on call next morning.

But always over and through all other tracks was a curious, delicate, lace-like fabric of polka-dots and interwoven sinuous lines. It was there each morning, fresh made the night before, whatever else was missing. But there was so much of its pattern that it was impossible to take any one line and follow it up.

At first it seemed to be made up of the trails of many small bipeds, each closely followed by its little one. Now, man and Birds are the only bipeds, but these were clearly not the tracks of any Bird. Trying to be judicial, I put together all the facts that the dust reported. First, here was proof that a number of tiny, two-legged, fur-slippered creatures came nightly to dance in the moonlight. Each one, as he pirouetted about, was closely followed by a much smaller one of the same kind, as though by his page. They came from nowhere and went again as they would. And they must have been invisible at will, or else how escape the ever-watchful Coyotes?

If only this had been in England or Ireland, any peasant could have explained it offhand – invisible pairs of tiny, furry boots, dancing in the moonlight – why, the veriest idiot knows that – *fairies*, of course.

But in New Mexico I had never heard of such a thing. In no work on this country, so far as I knew, was there any mention of their occurrence.

If only it could be! Would it not be delightful? I would gladly have believed. Christian Andersen would have insisted on believing in it, and then made others believe it, too. But for me, alas! it was impossible, for long ago, when my soul came to the fork in the trail marked on the left 'To Arcadie', on the right 'To Scientia', I took the flinty, upland right-hand path. I had given up my fayland eyes for – for I do not know what. And so I was puzzled, but the more puzzled, the more interested, of course; and remembering, from former experience, that it pays to offer a great deal of clear writing-space to the visitors who nightly favoured me with their autographs, I made with unusual care a large extension of the cleanswept dust sheet, to which the sage-brush-scented evening wind added a still smoother finish, and which next day enabled me to follow out a single line of the point-lace pattern.

It went dimpling down the path, towards the six old

corn-stumps called the garden, and then, leaving the clear written dust, it had turned aside, and seemed to end at a weed-covered mound, about which were several small holes that went in, not downward, but at a level. (Yes, of course, another pretty mystery nearly gone. How sharp the flints are on this upland path!) I set a trap by these holes, and next morning I had surely caught my 'fairy'. Just the loveliest, daintiest fawn-brown little creature that ever was seen in fur: large beautiful eyes like a Fawn's – no, not like a Fawn's, for no Fawn that ever lived had such wonderfully innocent orbs of liquid brown, ears like thinnest shells of the sea, showing the pink veins' flood of life. His hind feet were large and strong; but his fore feet – his hands, I mean – were the tiniest of the tiny, pinky white and rounded and dimpled, just like a baby's, only whiter and smaller than the tip of baby's smallest finger. His throat and breast were snowy white. However does he keep himself so sweetly clean in such a land of mud! Down the outside of his brown velvet knickerbockers was the cutest little silvery-white stripe, just like that on a trooper's breeches. His tail, the train that I suppose the page carried in dancing, was remarkably long, and was decorated to match the breeches with two long white stripes, and ended in a feather duster, which was very pretty but rather overdone, I thought, until I found out that it was designed for several important purposes.

His movements were just like what one might have expected from such an elegant creature. He had touched my heart before I had seen anything but his tracks, and now he won it wholly at first meeting.

'You little beauty! You have been so invisible and mysterious that I began to hope you were a fairy, but now I see I have heard of you before. You are *Perodipus ordi*, that is sometimes called the Kangaroo Rat. I am much obliged to you for all the lace designs you have sketched and for the pretty verses you have written for me, although I could not read them all; but I am eager to have you translate them, and, in fact, am ready to sit at those microscopic and beautiful feet of yours and learn.'

II

It is of course well known that the daintiest flowers grow out of the dirt, so I was not surprised to find that the Perodipus's home is in a cave underground. No doubt those wonderful eyes and long feelers were to help him in the unlighted corridors of his subterranean house.

It may seem a ruthless deed, but I was so eager to know him better that I determined to open his nest to the light of day as well as keep him a prisoner for a time, to act as my professor in Natural History.

I transferred the plush-clad atom of life to a large box that was lined with tin and half full of loose earth. Then I went out with a spade, carefully to follow and pry into the secrets of the Brownie world of which my captive was a native.

First I made a scaled diagram of the landscape concerned, for science is measurement, and exact knowledge was what I had sought since I made my choice of trails. Then I sketched the plants on the low mound. There were three large, prickly thistles, and two vigorous Spanish bayonets, or soapweeds, all of them dangerous to an unwary intruder. Next, I noticed there were nine gateways. Nine – I wonder why nine. Nine Muses? Nine lives? No, nothing of that sort (Perodipus does not live in the clouds). There were nine simply because in this case there happened to be nine direct approaches to this Perodipus's citadel. Another might have had three, or yet another twenty-three entries, according to the needs of its owner or the locality.

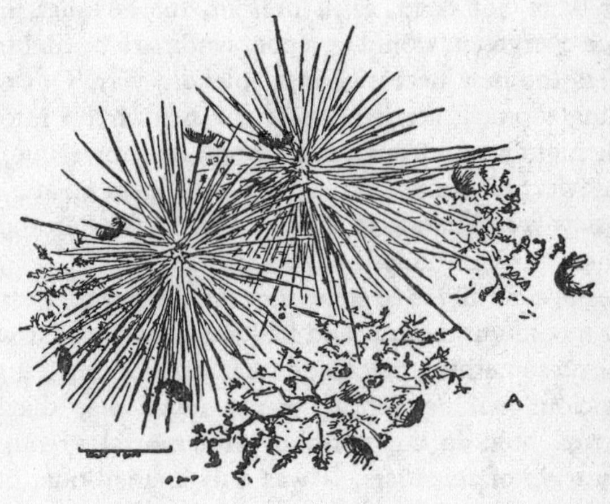

Over each of the nine holes was a strong, spine-armed sentinel forever on guard and absolutely unbuyable, so that if at any time the Coyote – the Satan of the little prairie-folk – should appear among the moonlight dancers, each could dash homeward and enter by a handy door, sure that there would be standing by that door a fearless, well-armed warden, who would say to the Coyote, in a language he would well understand, 'Stop! Keep off, or I'll spear you!'

And I feel very sure now that if an accident had opened a new approach, say in the direction of A, the wise little creature would also have made a handy door there for his own use. The Spanish bayonet could also keep the cattle and other heavy animals from trampling the mound, and when at night the Perodipus was making a dash for home with some fleet foe behind him, the tall, dark form of the friendly bayonet would be his landmark in the uncertain light. In summer-time, I now remembered, when other plants were not dead, as at present, the bayonet, in its sombre evergreen, would be a poor landmark by night; but it meets the new necessity in a splendid way. Out of its bristling topmost serried spears it sends far up into the purple night a wondrous candelabrum on a towering pole, with flowers of shining white, that must loom up afar, like some new constellation in the sky. And so the Perodipus's safety-port is lighthoused day and night.

I began carefully to open up the main gallery to the home of my moonlight dancer, and had not gone very far when I came on something that made me jump; nothing less than a ferocious-looking reptile – the *Huajalote*, that the Mexicans hold in superstitious and mortal dread, the *Amblystoma* of scientists. It was only a small one, but it gave me the creeps to see him lashing his venomous-looking tail and oozing all over with a poisonous slime. If he could affect me so much, what might he be like to the gentle little Perodipus, whose home he seemed trying to raid? But for some reason that I did not understand then, the reptile was boring his nose into a solid bank of sand that was the end of the gallery he had entered by. Since we were all playing 'fairy-tale', I, the Giant, did not hesitate to put the Dragon where he could harm the fairies no longer.

After hours of patient digging and measuring I got a map of the underground world where the Perodipus passes the daytime.

The central chamber could be *nearly* reached by any of the entrances, but one not knowing the secret would have passed by and come out into the air again at another door:

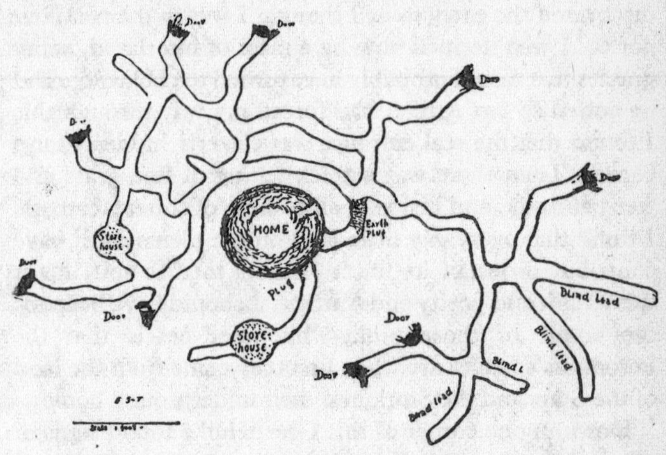

No matter how often he went in, he never would have found the nest or any of the real treasure of the home, for the road to the nest was plugged with earth each time the owner left it.

And this is exactly what happened to the Huajalote; for he seemed to have an idea that there was a secret passage if he only could find it, and no doubt thought it was somewhere through the bank of earth he was boring into, though really he was not anywhere near to the spot.

I think the chamber was not shut off from the air, for the small round hole X (see page 141) was, I suspect, its air-shaft, though I am not sure of this, for the roof caved in before I could examine it fully.

The chamber itself was very large, being twelve inches long and eight inches wide, with a high vaulted roof at least over five inches from the floor, and ribbed with the living roots of the grand old bayonet-trees at the door. Having discovered the entry to it, I thought I was in the nest; but not so. I was stopped now by a mass of interlaced, spiny grasses that would probably have turned the Huajalote had he gotten so far. After I had forced my way through this I found that the real entrance was cleverly hidden near a corner. Then there was a thick felting of fine grass and weed and silk, and inside of all a lining of softest feathers. I think that every gay little Bird on the plains must have contributed one of its finest feathers to that nest, for it was as soft and pretty and warm as it should have been for the cradle of those pinky-white seed-pearls that the Perodipus's babies are when first they come from the land of the Stars and the Stork into their underground home.

Down in one corner of this Great Hall I found signs of another secret passage. It was like exploring a medieval castle. This passage went down at a slant when I got fairly into it, and before long it opened out into a large storehouse that was filled with over a pint of seeds of the prairie sunflower. This room was sunken deepest of all in the ground, and was also in the shadiest part of the mound, so that the seed would be in no danger of heating or sprouting. At one end of this chamber was another blind lead that possibly was used in filling the warehouse and afterwards sealed up for safety. There were many of these blind alleys. They appeared to be either entrances plugged up or else deliberate plans to mislead an intruder who did not have the key to the secret door.

Yet one more chamber was found, and that was a second storehouse, a reserve supply of carefully selected helianthus seeds, about half a gill of them, and yet not a bad one or a shrivelled one was to be found in the lot.

But I did not find any of the Perodipus family, and think

it possible that when they heard my rude approach they all escaped by some other secret passage that I failed to discover.

This was the home of my nightly visitor, planned and carried out with wisdom for all the straits of his daily life and near future.

III

Its owner in the cage I now watched with double interest. He was the embodiment of restless energy, palpitating with life from the tip of his translucent nose and ears to the end of his vibrant tail. He could cross the box at a single bound, and I now saw the purpose of his huge tail. In the extraordinary long flying leaps that Perodipus makes, the tuft on the end does for him what the feathers do for an arrow. It keeps him straight in the air on his trajectory. But it does more, for it enables him slightly to change his course if he finds it wiser after he has leaped. And the tail itself has other uses. The Perodipus has no pocket in his striped trousers to carry home his winter supplies, but he has capacious pockets, one in each cheek, which he can fill till they bulge out wider than himself – so wide that he must turn his head sidewise to enter his own front gate. Such a load added to his head totally displaces his centre of gravity, which is adjusted for leaping with empty pockets. But here is where the tail comes in. Its great length and size make it a powerful lever, and by raising it to different angles he accommodates himself to his load and leaps along in perfect poise in spite of a week's provision in his cheeks.

He was the most indefatigable little miner that I ever saw. Those pinky-white paws, not much larger than a pencil-point, seemed never weary of digging, and would send the earth out between his hind legs in little jets like a steam-shovel. He seemed tireless at his work. He first tunnelled the whole mass through and through, and, I doubt not, made and unmade several ideal underground residences, and solved many problems of rapid underground transit. Then he embarked in some landscape-gardening schemes and made it his nightly business to change entirely the geography of his whole country, laboriously making hills and cañons wheresoever seemed unto him good.

There was one landscape effect that he seemed very fond of. That was a sort of Colorado Cañon with the San Francisco Mountain on its edge. He tried a long time to use a certain large stone for a peak to his mountain, but it was past his strength, and he resented, rather than profited by, any help I gave him. This stone gave him endless trouble for a time. He could not use it, nor even get rid of it, until he discovered that he could at least dig the earth from under it, and so keep it going down, until finally it settled at the bottom of the box and troubled him no more.

He used to take a lot of comfort out of jumping clear from the top of the Frisco Peak across the Grand Cañon into Utah (two hundred miles), at the other side of the box, and back home again to the Peak (six thousand feet).

I watched, sketched, and studied him as well as I could, considering his shyness and nocturnal habits, and I learned daily to admire him more. His untiring devotion to his nightly geographical lesson was marvellous. His talent for heaving up new mountain-ranges was astonishing, positively volcanic. When first I suspected his existence, I had been willing to call him a fairy. When I saw him I said, 'Why, it's only a Kangaroo Rat.' But after I had watched him a couple of weeks in the cage I realized fully that millions of little creatures with such energy, working for thousands of years, could not but change the whole surface of a country, by letting in the frost and rain, as well as by their own work. Then I was obliged to concede that Perodipus was more than Rat or Brownie; he was nothing less than a Geological Epoch.

IV

There was one more lesson, a great surprise, in store for me. It is well known to scientists that the common House-mouse has a song not unlike that of some Birds. Occasionally gifted individuals are found that fill our closet or cellar with midnight music that a Canary might be proud of. Further investigations have shown that the common Deer-mouse of the Eastern woods also is a gifted vocalist.

Now, any cowboy on the upland plains will tell you that at night, when sleeping out, he has often heard the most curious strains of birdy music in his half-awakening hours – a soft, sweet twittering song with trills and deeper notes – and if he thought about it at all he set it down to some small Bird singing in its dreams, or accepted his comrade's unexplanatory explanation that it was one of those 'prairie nightingales'. But what that was he did not trouble himself to know.

I have often heard the strange night song, but not being able to trace it home, I set it down to some little Bird that was too happy to express it all in daylight hours.

Several times at night I overheard from my captive a long-drawn note, before it dawned on me that this was the same voice as that which often sings to the rising moon. I did not hear him really sing, I am sorry to say. I have no final proof. My captive was not seeking to amuse me. Indeed, his attitude towards me from first to last was one of unbending scorn. I can only say I *think* (and hope) that it was the same voice. But my allegiance is due to exact science. Oh, why did I not take the other trail? For then I should have been able to announce here, as now I do not dare to, that the sweet night singer of the plains and the plush-clad fairy that nightly danced about my door *are the same.*

But one night there was a fresh upheaval of Nature, and my Immeasurable Force tried a new experiment in terrestrial convulsions. He started his mountain, not in the middle of his kingdom, as aforetime, but afar to the southwest, in one corner of the box, and a notable mountain he made. He simply ruined the Grand Cañon to use the material of its walls.

Higher and higher those tiny pink pawlets piled the beetling crags, and the dizzy peak arose above the sinking plain as it never had before.

It went up fast, too, for it was in the angle of the box, and it was rapidly nearing the heaven of heavens represented by the lid, when an accident turned the current of the Perodipus's ambitions. He was now at an altitude that he had never before reached since his imprisonment, so high that he could touch the narrow strip of the wooden walls that was unprotected by the tin. The new substance tempted his teeth. Oh, new-found joy! it was easy to cut. He set to work with his usual energy, and in a very short time cut his way through the half-inch pine, then escaped from the tin-clad kingdom that had been forced upon him, and its Geological Epoch was gone. My professor had quit his chair. I had been willing to find an impossible mystery, but I had found a delightful story from Nature's wonderland.

V

And now he is once more skimming merrily over the mud and sands of the upland plains; shooting across the open like a living, feathered arrow; tempting the rash Coyote to thrust his unfortunate nose into those awful cactus brakes, or teaching the Prairie Owls that if they do not let him alone they will surely come to grief on a Spanish bayonet; coming out by night again to scribble his lacework designs on the smooth places, to write verses of measured rhythm, or to sing and play hop-scotch in the moonlight with his merry crew.

Soft as a shadow, swift as an arrow, dainty as thistle-down, bright-eyed and beautiful, with a secret way to an underground world where he finds safety from his foes – my first impression was not so very far astray. I had surely found the Little Folk, and nearer, better, and more human Little Folk than any in the nursery books. My chosen flinty track had led me on to Upper Arcadie at last. And now, when I hear certain purblind folk talk of Fairies and Brownies as a race peculiar to the romantic parts of England, Ireland, or India, I think:

'*You* have been wasting your time reading books. You have never been on the shifting Currumpaw when the moon of the Mesas comes up to glint the river at its every bend, and bathe the hills in green and veil the shades in blue. You have not heard the moonlight music. You have not seen these moonbeams skip from thistle-top and bayonet-spear to rest in peace at last, as by appointment, on the smooth-swept dancing-floor of a tiny race that visits this earth each night, coming from nowhere, and disappearing without a sound of falling feet.

'You have never seen this, for you have not found the key

to the secret chamber; and if you did, you still might doubt, for the dainty moonlight revellers have coats of darkness and become invisible at will.

'Indeed, I believe you would say the whole thing was a dream. But what about the lace traceries in the dust? They are there when the sun comes up next morning.'

The Well-meaning Skunk

I have a profound admiration for the Skunk. Indeed, I once maintained that this animal was the proper emblem of America. It is, first of all, peculiar to this continent. It has stars on its head and stripes on its body. It is an ideal citizen; minds its own business, harms no one, and is habitually inoffensive, as long as it is left alone; but it will face any one or any number when aroused. It has a wonderful natural ability to take the offensive; and no man ever yet came to grips with a Skunk without being sadly sorry for it afterwards.

Nevertheless, in spite of all this, and the fact that several other countries have prior claims on the Eagle, I could not secure, for my view, sufficient popular support to change the national emblem.

From Atlantic to Pacific and from Mexico far north into the wilds of Canada the Skunk is found, varying with climate in size and colour indeed, but everywhere the same in character and in mode of defence.

It abounds in the broken country that lies between forest and prairie, but seems to avoid the thicker woods as well as the higher peaks.

In Yellowstone Park it is not common, but is found occasionally about Mammoth Hot Springs and Yancey's, at which latter place I had much pleasant acquaintance with its kind.

HIS SMELL-GUN

Every one knows that the animal can make a horrible smell in defending itself, but most persons do not realize what the smell is, or how it is made. First of all, and this should be in capitals, it has nothing at all to do with the kidneys or with the sex organs. It is simply a highly specialized musk secreted by a gland, or rather, a pair of them, located under the tail. It is used for defence when the Skunk is in peril of his life, or thinks he is. But a Skunk may pass his whole life without using it.

He can throw it to a distance of seven to ten feet according to his power or the wind. If it reaches the eyes of his assailant it blinds him temporarily. If it enters his mouth it sets up a frightful nausea. If the vapour gets into his lungs, it chokes as well as nauseates. There are cases on record of men and dogs being permanently blinded by this awful spray. And there is one case of a boy being killed by it.

Most Americans know somewhat of its terrors, but few of them realize the harmlessness of the Skunk when let alone. In remote places I find men who still think that this creature goes about shooting as wildly and wantonly as any drunken cowboy.

THE CRUELTY OF STEEL TRAPS

A few days ago while walking with a friend in the woods

we came on a Skunk. My companion shouted to the dog and captured him to save him from a possible disaster, then called to me to keep back and let the Skunk run away. But the fearless one in sable and ermine did not run, and I did not keep back, but I walked up very gently. The Skunk stood his ground and raised his tail high over his back, the sign of fight. I talked to him, still drawing nearer; then, when only ten feet away, was surprised to see that one of his feet was in a trap and terribly mangled.

I stooped down, saying many pleasant things about my friendliness, etc. The Skunk's tail slowly lowered and I came closer up. Still, I did not care to handle the wild and tormented thing on such short acquaintance, so I got a small barrel and quietly placed it over him, then removed the trap and brought him home, where he is now living in peace and comfort.

I mention this to show how gentle and judicious a creature the Skunk is when gently and judiciously approached. It is a sad commentary on our modes of dealing with wild life when I add that as afterwards appeared this Skunk had been struggling in the tortures of that trap for three days and three nights.

FRIENDLINESS OF THE SKUNK

These remarks are preliminary to an account of my adventures with a family of Skunks in the Park. During the summer I spent in the little shanty still to be seen opposite Yancey's, I lost no opportunity of making animal investigations. One of my methods was to sweep the dust on the trail and about the cabin quite smooth at night so that any creature passing should leave me his tracks and I should be sure that they were recent.

One morning on going out I found the fresh tracks of a Skunk. Next night these were seen again, in fact, there were two sets of them. A day or so later the cook at the nearby log hotel announced that a couple of Skunks came every evening to feed at the garbage bucket outside the kitchen door. That night I was watching for them. About dusk one came, walking along sedately with his tail at half mast. The house dog and the house cat both were at the door as the Skunk arrived. They glanced at the newcomer; then the cat discreetly went indoors and the dog rumbled in his chest, but discreetly he walked away, very stiffly, and looked at the distant landscape, with his hair on his back still bristling. The Skunk waddled up to the garbage pail, climbed in, though I was but ten feet away, and began his evening meal.

Another came later. Their tails were spread and at each sharp noise rose a little higher, but no one offered them harm, and they went their way when they were filled.

After this it was a regular thing to go out and see the Skunks feed when evening came.

PHOTOGRAPHING SKUNKS AT SHORT RANGE

I was anxious to get a picture or two, but was prevented by the poor light; in fact, it was but half light, and in those days we had no brilliant flash powders. So there was but one thing to do, that was trap my intended sitters.

Next night I was ready for them with an ordinary box trap, and even before the appointed time we saw a fine study in black and white come marching around the cow stable with banner-tail aloft, and across the grass towards the kitchen. The box trap was all ready and we – two women including my wife, and half a dozen men of the mountaineer type – were watching. The cat and the dog moved sullenly aside. The Skunk, with the calm confidence of one accustomed to respect, sniffed his way to the box trap with its tempting odorous bait. A Mink or a Marten, not to say a Fox, would have investigated a little before entering. The Skunk indulged in no such waste of time. What had he to fear – he the little lord of all things with the power of smell? He went in like one going home, seized the bait, and down went the door. The uninitiated onlookers expected an explosion from the Skunk, but I knew quite well he never wasted a shot, and did not hesitate to approach and make all safe. Now I wanted to move the box with its captive to my photographic studio, but could not carry it alone, so I asked the mountaineers to come and help. Had I asked them to join me in killing a man, shooting up the town, or otherwise taking their lives in their hands, I would doubtless have had half a dozen cheerful volunteers; but to carry a box in which was a wild Skunk – 'not for a hundred dollars', and the warriors melted into the background.

Then I said to my wife, 'Haven't *you* got nerve enough to help with this box? I'll guarantee that nothing will happen.' So she came and we took the box to my prepared enclosure, where next day I photographed him to my heart's content. More than once as I worked around at a distance of six or eight feet, the Skunk's tail flew up, but I kept perfectly still then; talked softly, apologizing and explaining: 'Now don't shoot at me. We are to be good friends. I wouldn't hurt you for anything. Now do drop that fighting flag, if you please, and be good.'

Gradually the tail went down and the captive looked at me in mere curiosity as I got my pictures.

I let him go by simply removing the wire netting of the fence, whereupon he waddled off under the cabin that I called 'home'.

WE SHARE THE SHANTY WITH THE SKUNKS

The next night as I lay in my bunk I heard a sniffing and scratching on the cabin floor. On looking over the edge of the bed I came face to face with my friend the Skunk. Our noses were but a foot apart and just behind him was another; I suppose his mate. I said: 'Hello! Here you are again. I'm glad to see you. Who's your friend?' He did not tell me, neither did he seem offended. I suppose it was his mate. That was the beginning of his residence under the floor of my cabin. My wife and I got very well acquainted with him and his wife before the summer was over. For though we had the cabin by day, the Skunks had it by night. We always left them some scraps, and regularly at dusk they came up to get them. They cleaned up our garbage, so helped to rid us of flies and mice. We were careful to avoid hurting or scaring our nightly visitors, so the summer passed without offence. We formed only the kindest feelings towards each other, and we left them in possession of the cabin, where, so far as I know, they are living yet, if you wish to call.

THE SKUNK AND THE UNWISE BOBCAT

As already noted, I swept the dust smooth around our shanty each night to make a sort of visitors' book. Then each morning I could go out and by study of the tracks get an exact idea of who had called. Of course there were many blank nights; on others the happenings were trifling, but some were full of interest. In this way I learned of the Coyote's visits to the garbage pail and of the Skunk establishment under the house, and other interesting facts.

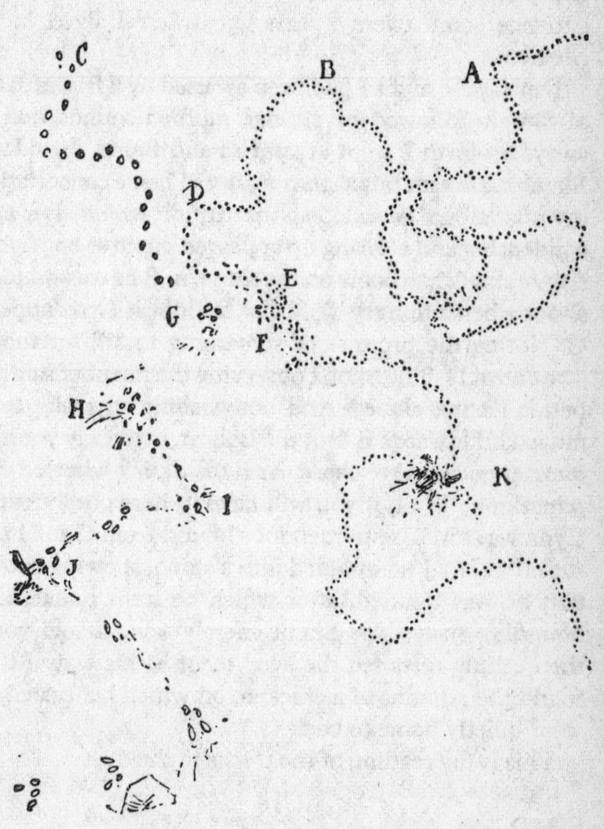

Track record of Bobcat's adventure with a skunk

I have always used this method of study in my mountain trips, and recall a most interesting record that rewarded my patience some twenty years ago when I lived in New Mexico.

During the night I had been aroused by a frightful smell of Skunk, followed by strange muffled sounds that died away. So forth I went at sunrise and found the odour of Skunk no dream but a stern reality. Then a consultation of my dust album revealed an inscription which after a little condensing and clearing up appeared much as on page 157. At A a skunk had come on the scene, at B he was wandering about when a hungry Wild Cat or Bobcat Lynx appeared, C. Noting the promise of something to kill for food, he came on at D. The Skunk observing the intruder said, 'You better let me alone.' And not wishing to make trouble moved off towards E. But the Bobcat, evidently young and inexperienced, gave chase. At F the Skunk wheeled about, remarking, 'Well, if you will have it, here goes!' At G the Lynx was hit. The tremendous bound from G to H shows the effect. At J he bumped into a stone, showing probably that he was blinded, after which he went bouncing and bounding away. The Skunk merely said, 'I told you so!' then calmly resumed the even tenor of his way. At K he found the remains of a chicken, on which he feasted, then went quietly home to bed.

This is my reading of the tracks in the dust.

MY PET SKUNKS

It would not be doing justice to the Skunk if I did not add a word about certain of the kind that I have at home.

For many years I have kept at least one pet Skunk. Just now I have about sixty. I keep them close to the house and would let them run loose indoors but for the possibility of some fool dog or cat coming around, and provoking the exemplary little brutes into a perfectly justifiable endeavour to defend themselves as nature taught them. But for this I should have no fear. Not only do I handle them myself, but I have induced many of my wild-eyed visitors to do so as a necessary part of their education. For few indeed there are in the land today that realize the gentleness and forbearance of this righteous little brother of ours, who, though armed with a weapon that will put the biggest and boldest to flight or disastrous defeat, yet refrains from using it until in absolute peril of his life, and then only after several warnings.

The Springfield Fox

I

The hens had been mysteriously disappearing for over a month; and when I came home to Springfield for the summer holidays it was my duty to find the cause. This was soon done. The fowls were carried away bodily one at a time, before going to roost or else after leaving, which put tramps and neighbours out of court; they were not taken from the high perches, which cleared all coons and owls; or left partly eaten, so that weasels, skunks, or minks were not the guilty ones, and the blame, therefore, was surely left at Reynard's door.

The great pine wood of Erindale was on the other bank of the river, and on looking carefully about the lower ford I saw a few fox-tracks and a barred feather from one of our Plymouth Rock chickens. On climbing the farther bank in search of more clues, I heard a great outcry of crows behind me, and turning, saw a number of these birds darting down at something in the ford. A better view showed that it was the old story, thief catch thief, for there in the middle of the ford was a fox with something in his jaws – he was returning from our barnyard with another hen. The crows, though shameless robbers themselves, are ever first to cry 'Stop thief', and yet more than ready to take 'hush-money' in the form of a share in the plunder.

And this was their game now. The fox to get back home must cross the river, where he was exposed to the full brunt of the crow mob. He made a dash for it, and would doubtless have gotten across with his booty had I not joined in the attack, whereupon he dropped the hen, scarce dead, and disappeared in the woods.

This large and regular levy of provisions wholly carried off could mean but one thing, a family of little foxes at home; and to find them I now was bound.

That evening I went with Ranger, my hound, across the river into the Erindale woods. As soon as the hound began to circle, we heard the short, sharp bark of a fox from a thickly wooded ravine close by. Ranger dashed in at once, struck a hot scent and went off on a lively straight-away till his voice was lost in the distance away over the upland.

After nearly an hour he came back, panting and warm, for it was baking August weather, and lay down at my feet.

But almost immediately the same foxy '*Yap yurrr*' was heard close at hand and off dashed the dog on another chase.

Away he went in the darkness, baying like a foghorn, straight away to the north. And the loud '*Boo, boo*', became a low '*oo, oo*', and that a feeble 'o-o' and then was lost. They must have gone some miles away, for even with ear to the ground I heard nothing of them though a mile was easy distance for Ranger's brazen voice.

As I waited in the black woods I heard a sweet sound of dripping water: '*Tink tank tenk tink, Ta tink tank tenk tonk.*'

I did not know of any spring so near, and in the hot night

it was a glad find. But the sound led me to the bough of an oak-tree, where I found its source. Such a soft sweet song; full of delightful suggestion on such a night:

Tonk tank tenk tink
Ta tink a tonk a tank a tink a
Ta ta tink tank ta ta tonk tink
Drink a tank a drink a drunk.

It was the 'water-dripping' song of the saw-whet owl.

But suddenly a deep raucous breathing and a rustle of leaves showed that Ranger was back. He was completely fagged out. His tongue hung almost to the ground and was dripping with foam, his flanks were heaving and spume-flecks dribbled from his breast and sides. He stopped panting a moment to give my hand a dutiful lick, then flung himself flop on the leaves to drown all other sounds with his noisy panting.

But again that tantalizing '*Yap yurrr*' was heard a few feet away, and the meaning of it all dawned on me.

We were close to the den where the little foxes were, and the old ones were taking turns in trying to lead us away.

It was late night now, so we went home feeling sure that the problem was nearly solved.

II

It was well known that there was an old fox with his family living in the neighbourhood, but no one supposed them so near.

This fox had been called 'Scarface', because of a scar reaching from his eye through and back of his ear; this was supposed to have been given him by a barbed-wire fence during a rabbit hunt, and as the hair came in white after it healed, it was always a strong mark.

The winter before I had met with him and had had a sample of his craftiness. I was out shooting, after a fall of snow, and had crossed the open fields to the edge of the brushy hollow back of the old mill. As my head rose to a view of the hollow I caught sight of a fox trotting at long range down the other side, in line to cross my course. Instantly I held motionless, and did not even lower or turn my head lest I should catch his eye by moving, until he went on out of sight in the thick cover at the bottom. As soon as he was hidden I bobbed down and ran to head him off where he should leave the cover on the other side, and was there in good time awaiting, but no fox came forth. A careful look showed the fresh track of a fox that had bounded from the cover, and following it with my eye I saw old Scarface himself far out of range behind me, sitting on his haunches and grinning as though much amused.

A study of the trail made all clear. He had seen me at the moment I saw him, but he, also like a true hunter, had concealed the fact, putting on an air of unconcern till out of sight, when he had run for his life around behind me and amused himself by watching my stillborn trick.

In the springtime I had yet another instance of Scarface's cunning. I was walking with a friend along the road over the high pasture. We passed within thirty feet of a ridge on which were several grey and brown boulders. When at the nearest point my friend said:

'Stone number three looks to me very much like a fox curled up.'

But I could not see it, and we passed. We had not gone many yards farther when the wind blew on this boulder as on fur.

My friend said, 'I am sure that is a fox, lying asleep.'

'We'll soon settle that,' I replied, and turned back, but as soon as I had taken one step from the road, up jumped Scarface, for it was he, and ran. A fire had swept the middle of the pasture, leaving a broad belt of black; over this he scurried till he came to the unburnt yellow grass again, where he squatted down and was lost to view. He had been watching us all the time, and would not have moved had we kept to the road. The wonderful part of this is, not that he resembled the round stones and dry grass, but that he *knew he did*, and was ready to profit by it.

We soon found that it was Scarface and his wife Vixen that had made our woods their home and our barnyard their base of supplies.

Next morning a search in the pines showed a great bank of earth that had been scratched up within a few months. It must have come from a hole, and yet there was none to be seen. It is well known that a really cute fox, on digging a new den, brings all the earth out at the first hole made, but carries on a tunnel into some distant thicket. Then closing up for good the first made and too well-marked door, uses only the entrance hidden in the thicket.

So after a little search at the other side of a knoll, I found the real entry and good proof that there was a nest of little foxes inside.

Rising above the brush on the hillside was a great hollow basswood. It leaned a good deal and had a large hole at the bottom, and a smaller one at top.

We boys had often used this tree in playing Swiss Family Robinson, and by cutting steps in its soft punky walls had made it easy to go up and down in the hollow. Now it came in handy, for next day when the sun was warm I went there to watch, and from this perch on the roof, I soon saw the interesting family that lived in the cellar near by. There were four little foxes; they looked curiously like little lambs, with their woolly coats, their long thick legs and innocent expressions, and yet a second glance at their broad, sharp-nosed, sharp-eyed visages showed that each of these innocents was the makings of a crafty old fox.

They played about, basking in the sun, or wrestling with each other till a slight sound made them scurry under ground. But their alarm was needless, for the cause of it was their mother; she stepped from the bushes bringing another hen – number seventeen as I remember. A low call from her and the little fellows came tumbling out. Then began a scene that I thought charming, but which my uncle would not have enjoyed at all.

They rushed on the hen, and tussled and fought with it, and each other, while the mother, keeping a sharp eye for enemies, looked on with fond delight. The expression on her face was remarkable. It was first a grinning of delight, but her usual look of wildness and cunning was there, nor were cruelty and nervousness lacking, but over all was the unmistakable look of the mother's pride and love.

The base of my tree was hidden in bushes and much lower than the knoll where the den was. So I could come and go at will without scaring the foxes.

For many days I went there and saw much of the training of the young ones. They early learned to turn to statuettes at any strange sound, and then on hearing it again or finding other cause for fear, to run for shelter.

Some animals have so much mother-love that it overflows and benefits outsiders. Not so old Vixen it would seem. Her pleasure in the cubs led to most refined cruelty. For she often brought home to them mice and birds alive, and with diabolic gentleness would avoid doing them serious hurt so that the cubs might have larger scope to torment them.

There was a woodchuck that lived over in the hill orchard. He was neither handsome nor interesting, but he knew how to take care of himself. He had dug a den between the roots of an old pine stump, so that the foxes could not follow him by digging. But hard work was not their way of life; wits they believed worth more than elbow-grease. This woodchuck usually sunned himself on the stump each morning. If he saw a fox near he went down in the door of his den, or if the enemy was very near he went inside and stayed long enough for the danger to pass.

One morning Vixen and her mate seemed to decide that it was time the children knew something about the broad subject of Woodchucks, and further that this orchard woodchuck would serve nicely for an object-lesson. So they went together to the orchard-fence unseen by old Chuckie on his stump. Scarface then showed himself in the orchard and quietly walked in a line so as to pass by the stump at a distance, but never once turned his head or allowed the ever-watchful woodchuck to think himself seen. When the fox entered the field the woodchuck quietly dropped down to the mouth of his den; here he waited as the fox passed, but concluding that after all wisdom is the better part, went into his hole.

This was what the foxes wanted. Vixen had kept out of sight, but now ran swiftly to the stump and hid behind it. Scarface had kept straight on, going very slowly. The woodchuck had not been frightened, so before long his head popped up between the roots and he looked around. There was that fox still going on, farther and farther away. The woodchuck grew bold as the fox went, and came out farther, and then seeing the coast clear, he scrambled on to the stump, and with one spring Vixen had him and shook him till he lay senseless. Scarface had watched out of the corner of his eye and now came running back. But Vixen took the chuck in her jaws and made for the den, so he saw he wasn't needed.

Back to the den came Vix, and carried the chuck so carefully that he was able to struggle a little when she got there. A low *'woof'* at the den brought the little fellows out like schoolboys to play. She threw the wounded animal to them and they set on him like four little furies, uttering little growls and biting little bites with all the strength of their baby jaws, but the woodchuck fought for his life and beating them off slowly hobbled to the shelter of a thicket. The little ones pursued like a pack of hounds and dragged at his tail and flanks, but could not hold him back. So Vix overtook him with a couple of bounds and dragged him again into the open for the children to worry. Again and again this rough sport went on till one of the little ones was badly bitten, and his squeal of pain roused Vix to end the woodchuck's misery and serve him up at once.

Not far from the den was a hollow overgrown with coarse grass, the playground of a colony of field-mice. The earliest lesson in woodcraft that the little ones took, away from the den, was in this hollow. Here they had their first course of mice, the easiest of all game. In teaching, the main thing was example, aided by a deep-set instinct. The old fox, also, had one or two signs meaning 'lie still and watch', 'come, do as I do', and so on, that were much used.

So the merry lot went to this hollow one calm evening and Mother Fox made them lie still in the grass. Presently a faint squeak showed that the game was astir. Vix rose up and went on tip-toe into the grass – not crouching but as high as she could stand, sometimes on her hind legs so as to get a better view. The runs that the mice follow are hidden under the grass tangle, and the only way to know the whereabouts of a mouse is by seeing the slight shaking of the grass, which is the reason why mice are hunted only on calm days.

And the trick is to locate the mouse and seize him first

and see him afterwards. Vix soon made a spring, and in the middle of the bunch of dead grass that she grabbed was a field-mouse squeaking his last squeak.

He was soon gobbled, and the four awkward little foxes tried to do the same as their mother, and when at length the eldest for the first time in his life caught game, he quivered with excitement and ground his pearly little milk-teeth into the mouse with a rush of inborn savageness that must have surprised even himself.

Another home lesson was on the red-squirrel. One of these noisy, vulgar creatures, lived close by and used to waste part of each day scolding the foxes, from some safe perch. The cubs made many vain attempts to catch him as he ran across their glade from one tree to another, or spluttered and scolded at them a foot or so out of reach. But old Vixen was up in natural history – she knew squirrel nature and took the case in hand when the proper time came. She hid the children and lay down flat in the middle of the open glade. The saucy low-minded squirrel came and scolded as usual. But she moved no hair. He came nearer and at last right overhead to chatter:

'You brute you, you brute you.'

But Vix lay as dead. This was very perplexing, so the squirrel came down the trunk and peeping about made a nervous dash across the grass, to another tree, again to scold from a safe perch.

'You brute you, you useless brute, scarrr-scarrrrr.'

But flat and lifeless on the grass lay Vix. This was most tantalizing to the squirrel. He was naturally curious and disposed to be venturesome, so again he came to the ground and scurried across the glade nearer than before.

Still as death lay Vix, 'surely she was dead'. And the little foxes began to wonder if their mother wasn't asleep.

But the squirrel was working himself into a little craze

of foolhardy curiosity. He had dropped a piece of bark on Vix's head, he had used up his list of bad words and he had done it all over again, without getting a sign of life. So after a couple more dashes across the glade he ventured within a few feet of the really watchful Vix, who sprang to her feet and pinned him in a twinkling.

'And the little ones picked the bones e-oh.'

Thus the rudiments of their education were laid, and afterwards as they grew stronger they were taken farther afield to begin the higher branches of trailing and scenting.

For each kind of prey they were taught a way to hunt, for every animal has some great strength or it could not live, and some great weakness or the others could not live. The squirrel's weakness was foolish curiosity; the fox's that he can't climb a tree. And the training of the little foxes was all shaped to take advantage of the weakness of the other creatures and to make up for their own by defter play where they are strong.

From their parents they learned the chief axioms of the fox world. How, is not easy to say. But that they learned this in company with their parents was clear. Here are some that foxes taught me, without saying a word: –

Never sleep on your straight track.

Your nose is before your eyes, then trust it first.

A fool runs down the wind.

Running rills cure many ills.

Never take the open if you can keep the cover.

Never leave a straight trail if a crooked one will do.

If it's strange, it's hostile.

Dust and water burn the scent.

Never hunt mice in a rabbit-woods, or rabbits in a hen-yard.

Keep off the grass.

Inklings of the meanings of these were already entering

the little ones' minds – thus, 'Never follow what you can't smell,' was wise, they could see, because if you can't smell it, then the wind is so that it must smell you.

One by one they learned the birds and beasts of their home woods, and then as they were able to go abroad with their parents they learned new animals. They were beginning to think they knew the scent of everything that moved. But one night the mother took them to a field where was a strange black flat thing on the ground. She brought them on purpose to smell it, but at the first whiff their every hair stood on end, they trembled, they knew not why – it seemed to tingle through their blood and fill them with instinctive hate and fear. And when she saw its full effect she told them –

'*That is man-scent.*'

III

Meanwhile the hens continued to disappear. I had not betrayed the den of cubs. Indeed, I thought a good deal more of the little rascals than I did of the hens; but uncle was dreadfully wrought up and made most disparaging remarks about my woodcraft. To please him I one day took the hound across to the woods and seating myself on a stump on the open hillside, I bade the dog go on. Within three minutes he sang out in the tongue all hunters know so well, 'Fox! fox! fox! straight away down the valley.'

After awhile I heard them coming back. There I saw the fox – Scarface – loping lightly across the river-bottom to the stream. In he went and trotted along in the shallow water near the margin for two hundred yards, then came out straight towards me. Though in full view, he saw me not but came up the hill watching over his shoulder for the hound. Within ten feet of me he turned and sat with his back to me while he craned his neck and showed an eager interest in the doings of the hound. Ranger came bawling along the trail till he came to the running water, the killer of scent, and here he was puzzled; but there was only one thing to do; that was by going up and down both banks to find where the fox had left the river.

The fox before me shifted his position a little to get a better view and watched with a most human interest all the circling of the hound. He was so close that I saw the hair of his shoulder bristle a little when the dog came in sight. I could see the jumping of his heart on his ribs, and the gleam of his yellow eye. When the dog was wholly baulked by the water trick, it was comical to see: – he could not sit still, but rocked up and down in glee, and reared on his hind feet to get a better view of the slow-plodding hound. With mouth opened nearly to his ears, though not at all winded, he panted noisily for a moment, or rather he laughed gleefully, just as a dog laughs by grinning and panting.

Old Scarface wriggled in huge enjoyment as the hound puzzled over the trail so long that when he did find it, it was so stale he could barely follow it, and did not feel justified in tonguing on it at all.

As soon as the hound was working up the hill, the fox quietly went into the woods. I had been sitting in plain view only ten feet away, but I had the wind and kept still and the fox never knew that his life had for twenty minutes been in the power of the foe he most feared. Ranger also would have passed me as near as the fox, but I spoke to him, and with a little nervous start he quit the trail and looking sheepish lay down by my feet.

This little comedy was played with variations for several days, but it was all in plain view from the house across the river. My uncle, impatient at the daily loss of hens, went out himself, sat in the open knoll, and when old Scarface trotted to his lookout to watch the dull hound on the river flat below, my uncle remorselessly shot him in the back, at the very moment when he was grinning over a new triumph.

IV

But still the hens were disappearing. My uncle was wrathy. He determined to conduct the war himself, and sowed the woods with poison baits, trusting to luck that our own dogs would not get them. He indulged in contemptuous remarks on my by-gone woodcraft, and went out evenings with a gun and the two dogs, to see what he could destroy.

Vix knew right well what a poisoned bait was; she passed them by or else treated them with active contempt, but one she dropped down the hole of an old enemy, a skunk, who was never afterwards seen. Formerly old Scarface was always ready to take charge of the dogs, and keep them out of mischief. But now that Vix had the whole burden of the brood, she could no longer spend time in breaking every track to the den, and was not always at hand to meet and mislead the foes that might be coming too near.

The end is easily foreseen. Ranger followed a hot trail to the den, and Spot, the fox-terrier, announced that the family was at home, and then did his best to go in after them.

The whole secret was now out, and the whole family doomed. The hired man came around with pick and shovel to dig them out, while we and the dogs stood by. Old Vix soon showed herself in the near woods, and led the dogs away off down the river, where she shook them off when she thought proper, by the simple device of springing on a sheep's back. The frightened animal ran for several hundred yards, then Vix got off, knowing that there was now a hopeless gap in the scent, and returned to the den. But the dogs, baffled by the break in the trail, soon did the same, to find Vix hanging about in despair, vainly trying to decoy us away from her treasures.

Meanwhile Paddy plied both pick and shovel with vigour and effect. The yellow, gravelly sand was heaping on both sides, and the shoulders of the sturdy digger were sinking below the level. After an hour's digging, enlivened by frantic rushes of the dogs after the old fox, who hovered near in the woods, Pat called:

'Here they are, sor!'

It was the den at the end of the burrow, and cowering as far back as they could, were the four little woolly cubs.

Before I could interfere, a murderous blow from the shovel, and a sudden rush for the fierce little terrier, ended the lives of three. The fourth and smallest was barely saved by holding him by his tail high out of reach of the excited dogs.

He gave one short squeal, and his poor mother came at the cry, and circled so near that she would have been shot but for the accidental protection of the dogs, who somehow always seemed to get between, and whom she once more led away on a fruitless chase.

The little one saved alive was dropped into a bag, where he lay quite still. His unfortunate brothers were thrown back into their nursery bed, and buried under a few shovelfuls of earth.

We guilty ones then went back into the house, and the little fox was soon chained in the yard. No one knew just why he was kept alive, but in all a change of feeling had set in, and the idea of killing him was without a supporter.

He was a pretty little fellow, like a cross between a fox

and a lamb. His woolly visage and form were strangely lamb-like and innocent, but one could find in his yellow eyes a gleam of cunning and savageness as unlamb-like as it possibly could be.

As long as anyone was near he crouched sullen and cowed in his shelter-box, and it was a full hour after being left alone before he ventured to look out.

My window now took the place of the hollow basswood. A number of hens of the breed he knew so well were about the cub in the yard. Late that afternoon as they strayed near the captive there was a sudden rattle of the chain, and the youngster dashed at the nearest one and would have caught him but for the chain which brought him up with a jerk. He got on his feet and slunk back to his box, and though he afterwards made several rushes he so gauged his leap to win or fail within the length of the chain and never again was brought up by its cruel jerk.

As night came down the little fellow became very uneasy, sneaking out of his box, but going back at each slight alarm, tugging at his chain, or at times biting it in fury while he held it down with his fore paws. Suddenly he paused as though listening, then raising his little black nose he poured out a short quavering cry.

Once or twice this was repeated, the time between being occupied in worrying the chain and running about. Then an answer came. The far-away *Yap-yurrr* of the old fox. A few minutes later a shadowy form appeared on the wood-pile. The little one slunk into his box, but at once returned and ran to meet his mother with all the gladness that a fox could show. Quick as a flash she seized him and turned to bear him away by the road she came. But the moment the end of the chain was reached the cub was rudely jerked from the old one's mouth, and she, scared by the opening of a window, fled over the wood-pile.

An hour afterwards the cub had ceased to run about or cry. I peeped out, and by the light of the moon saw the form of the mother at full length on the ground by the little one, gnawing at something – the clank of iron told what, it was that cruel chain. And Tip, the little one, meanwhile was helping himself to a warm drink.

On my going out she fled into the dark woods, but there by the shelter-box were two little mice, bloody and still warm, food for the cub brought by the devoted mother. And in the morning I found the chain was very bright for a foot or two next the little one's collar.

On walking across the woods to the ruined den, I again found signs of Vixen. The poor heart-broken mother had come and dug out the bedraggled bodies of her little ones.

There lay the three little baby foxes all licked smooth now, and by them were two of our hens fresh killed. The newly heaved earth was printed all over with tell-tale signs – signs that told me that here by the side of her dead she had watched like Rizpah. Here she had brought their usual meal, the spoil of her nightly hunt. Here she had stretched herself beside them and vainly offered them their natural drink and yearned to feed and warm them as of old; but only stiff little bodies under their soft wool she found, and little cold noses still and unresponsive.

A deep impress of elbows, breast, and hocks showed where she had laid in silent grief and watched them for long and mourned as a wild mother can mourn for its young. But from that time she came no more to the ruined den, for now she surely knew that her little ones were dead.

V

Tip the captive, the weakling of the brood, was now the heir to all her love. The dogs were loosed to guard the hens. The hired man had orders to shoot the old fox on sight – so had I, but was resolved never to see her. Chicken-heads, that a fox loves and a dog will not touch, had been poisoned and scattered through the woods; and the only way to the yard where Tip was tied, was by climbing the wood-pile after braving all other dangers. And yet each night old Vix was there to nurse her baby and bring it fresh-killed hens and game. Again and again I saw her, although she came now without awaiting the querulous cry of the captive.

The second night of the captivity I heard the rattle of the chain, and then made out that the old fox was there, hard at work digging a hole by the little one's kennel. When it was deep enough to half bury her, she gathered into it all the slack of the chain, and filled it again with earth. Then in triumph thinking she had gotten rid of the chain, she seized little Tip by the neck and turned to dash off up the wood-pile, but alas! only to have him jerked roughly from her grasp.

Poor little fellow, he whimpered sadly as he crawled into his box. After half an hour there was a great outcry among the dogs, and by their straight-away tonguing through the far woods I knew they were chasing Vix. Away up north they went in the direction of the railway and their noise faded from hearing. Next morning the hound had not come back. We soon knew why. Foxes long ago learned what a railroad is; they soon devised several ways of turning it to account. One way is when hunted to walk the rails for a long distance just before a train comes. The scent, always poor on iron, is destroyed by the train and there is always a chance of hounds being killed by the engine. But another way more sure, but harder to play, is to lead the hounds straight to a high trestle just ahead of the train, so that the engine overtakes them on it and they are surely dashed to destruction.

This trick was skilfully played, and down below we found the mangled remains of old Ranger and learned that Vix was already wreaking her revenge.

. That same night she returned to the yard before Spot's weary limbs could bring him back and killed another hen and brought it to Tip, and stretched her panting length beside him that he might quench his thirst. For she seemed to think he had no food but what she brought.

It was that hen that betrayed to my uncle the nightly visits.

My own sympathies were all turning to Vix, and I would have no hand in planning further murders. Next night my uncle himself watched, gun in hand, for an hour. Then when it became cold and the moon clouded over he remembered other important business elsewhere, and left Paddy in his place.

But Paddy was 'onaisy' as the stillness and anxiety of watching worked on his nerves. And the loud bang! bang! an hour later left us sure only that powder had been burned.

In the morning we found Vix had not failed her young one. Again next night found my uncle on guard, for another hen had been taken. Soon after dark a single shot was heard, but Vix dropped the game she was bringing and escaped. Another attempt made that night called forth another gunshot. Yet next day it was seen by the brightness of the chain that she had come again and vainly tried for hours to cut that hateful bond.

Such courage and staunch fidelity were bound to win respect, if not toleration. At any rate, there was no gunner in wait next night, when all was still. Could it be of any use? Driven off thrice with gun-shots, would she make another try to feed or free her captive young one?

Would she? Hers was a mother's love. There was but one to watch them this time, the fourth night, when the quavering whine of the little one was followed by that shadowy form above the wood-pile.

But carrying no fowl or food that could be seen. Had the keen huntress failed at last? Had she no head of game for this her only charge, or had she learned to trust his captors for his food?

No, far from all this. The wild-wood mother's heart and hate were true. Her only thought had been to set him free. All means she knew she tried, and every danger braved to tend him well and help him to be free. But all had failed.

Like a shadow she came and in a moment was gone, and Tip seized on something dropped, and crunched and chewed with relish what she brought. But even as he ate, a knife-like pang shot through and a scream of pain escaped him. Then there was a momentary struggle and the little fox was dead.

The mother's love was strong in Vix, but a higher thought was stronger. She knew right well the poison's power; she knew the poison bait, and would have taught him had he lived to know and shun it too. But now at last when she must choose for him a wretched prisoner's life or sudden death, she quenched the mother in her breast and freed him by the one remaining door.

It is when the snow is on the ground that we take the census of the woods, and when the winter came it told me that Vix no longer roamed the woods of Erindale. Where she went it never told, but only this, that she was gone.

Gone, perhaps, to some other far-off haunt to leave behind the sad remembrance of her murdered little ones and mate. Or gone, may be, deliberately, from the scene of a sorrowful life, as many a wild-wood mother has gone, by the means that she herself had used to free her young one, the last of all her brood.

The Slum Cat

LIFE I

I

'M-E-A-T! M-E-A-T!' came shrilling down Scrimper's Alley. Surely the Pied Piper of Hamelin was there, for it seemed that all the Cats in the neighbourhood were running towards the sound, though the Dogs, it must be confessed, looked scornfully indifferent.

'Meat! Meat!' and louder; then the centre of attraction came in view – a rough, dirty little man with a push-cart; while straggling behind him were a score of Cats that joined in his cry with a sound nearly the same as his own. Every fifty yards, that is, as soon as a goodly throng of Cats was gathered, the push-cart stopped. The man with the magic voice took out of the box in his cart a skewer on which were pieces of strong-smelling boiled liver. With a long stick he pushed pieces off. Each Cat seized on one, and wheeling, with a slight depression of the ears and a little tiger growl and glare, she rushed away with her prize to devour it in some safe retreat.

'Meat! Meat!' And still they came to get their portions.

All were well known to the meat-man. There was Castiglione's Tiger; this was Jones's Black; here was Pralitsky's 'Torkershell', and this was Madame Danton's White; there sneaked Blenkinshoff's Maltee, and that climbing on the barrow was Sawyer's old Orange Billy, an impudent fraud that never had had any financial backing – all to be remembered and kept in account. This one's owner was sure pay, a dime a week; that one's doubtful. There was John Washee's Cat, that got only a small piece because John was in arrears. Then there was the saloon-keeper's collared and ribboned ratter, which got an extra lump because the 'barkeep' was liberal; and the roundsman's Cat, that brought no cash, but got unusual consideration because the meat-man did. But there were others. A black Cat with a white nose came rushing confidently with the rest, only to be repulsed savagely. Alas! Pussy did not understand. She had been a pensioner of the barrow for months. Why this unkind change? It was beyond her comprehension. But the meat-man knew. Her mistress had stopped payment. The meat-man kept no books but his memory, and it was never at fault.

Outside the patrician 'four hundred' about the barrow, were other Cats, keeping away from the push-cart because they were not on the list, the Social Register as it were, yet fascinated by the heavenly smell and the faint possibility of accidental good luck. Among these hangers-on was a thin grey Slummer, a homeless Cat that lived by her wits – slab-sided and not over-clean. One could see at a glance that she was doing her duty by a family in some out-of-the-way corner. She kept one eye on the barrow circle and the other on the possible Dogs. She saw a score of happy Cats slink off with their delicious 'daily' and their tiger-like air, but no opening for her, till a big Tom of her own class sprang on a little pensioner with intent to rob. The victim dropped the meat to defend herself against the enemy, and before the 'all-powerful' could intervene, the grey Slummer saw her chance, seized the prize, and was gone.

She went through the hole in Menzie's side door and over the wall at the back, then sat down and devoured the lump of liver, licked her chops, felt absolutely happy, and set out by devious ways to the rubbish-yard, where, in the bottom of an old cracker-box, her family was awaiting her. A plaintive mewing reached her ears. She went at speed and reached the box to see a huge Black Tom-cat calmly destroying her brood. He was twice as big as she, but she went at him with all her strength, and he did as most animals will do when caught wrong-doing, he turned and ran away. Only one was left, a little thing like its mother, but of more pronounced colour – grey with black spots, and a white touch on nose, ears, and tail-tip. There can be no question of the mother's grief for a few days; but that wore off, and all her care was for the survivor. That benevolence was as far as possible from the motives of the murderous old Tom there can be no doubt; but he proved a blessing in deep disguise, for both mother and Kit were visibly bettered in a short time. The daily quest for food continued. The meat-man rarely proved a success, but the ash-cans were there, and if they did not afford a meat-supply, at least they were sure to produce potato-skins that could be used to allay the gripe of hunger for another day.

One night the mother Cat smelt a wonderful smell that came from the East River at the end of the alley. A new smell always needs investigating, and when it is attractive as well as new, there is but one course open. It led Pussy to the docks a block away, and then out on a wharf, away from any cover but the night. A sudden noise, a growl and a rush, were the first notice she had that she was cut off by her old enemy, the Wharf Dog. There was only one escape.

She leaped from the wharf to the vessel from which the smell came. The Dog could not follow, so when the fish-boat sailed in the morning Pussy unwillingly went with her and was seen no more.

II

The Slum Kitten waited in vain for her mother. The morning came and went. She became very hungry. Towards evening a deep-laid instinct drove her forth to seek food. She slunk out of the old box, and feeling her way silently among the rubbish, she smelt everything that seemed eatable, but without finding food. At length she reached the wooden steps leading down into Jap Malee's bird-store underground. The door was open a little. She wandered into a world of rank and curious smells and a number of living things in cages all about her. A negro was sitting idly on a box in a corner. He saw the little stranger enter and watched it curiously. It wandered past some Rabbits. They paid no heed. It came to a wide-barred cage in which was a Fox. The gentleman with the bushy tail was in a far corner. He crouched low; his eyes glowed. The Kitten wandered, sniffing, up to the bars, put its head in, sniffed again, then made towards the feedpan, to be seized in a flash by the crouching Fox. It gave a frightened 'mew', but a single shake cut that short and would have ended Kitty's nine lives at once, had not the negro come to the rescue. He had no weapon and could not get into the cage, but he spat with such copious vigour in the Fox's face that he dropped the Kitten and returned to the corner, there to sit blinking his eyes in sullen fear.

The negro pulled the Kitten out. The shake of the beast of prey seemed to have stunned the victim, really to have saved it much suffering. The Kitten seemed unharmed, but giddy. It tottered in a circle for a time, then slowly revived, and a few minutes later was purring in the negro's lap, apparently none the worse, when Jap Malee, the bird-man, came home.

Jap was not an Oriental; he was a full-blooded Cockney, but his eyes were such little accidental slits aslant in his round, flat face, that his first name was forgotten in the highly descriptive title of 'Jap'. He was not especially unkind to the birds and beasts whose sales were supposed to furnish his living, but his eye was on the main chance; he knew what he wanted. He didn't want the Slum Kitten.

The negro gave it all the food it could eat, then carried it to a distant block and dropped it in a neighbouring iron-yard.

III

One full meal is as much as any one needs in two or three days, and under the influence of this stored-up heat and power, Kitty was very lively. She walked around the piled-up rubbish, cast curious glances on far-away Canary-birds in cages that hung from high windows; she peeped over fences, discovered a large Dog, got quietly down again, and presently finding a sheltered place in full sunlight, she lay down and slept for an hour. A slight 'sniff' awakened her, and before her stood a large Black Cat with glowing green eyes, and the thick neck and square jaws that distinguish the Tom; a scar marked his cheek, and his left ear was torn. His look was far from friendly; his ears moved backwards a little, his tail twitched, and a faint, deep sound came from his throat. The Kitten innocently walked towards him. She did not remember him. He rubbed the sides of his jaws on a post, and quietly, slowly turned and disappeared. The last that she saw of him was the end of his tail twitching from side to side; and the little Slummer had no idea that she had been as near death today, as she had been when she ventured into the fox-cage.

As night came on the Kitten began to feel hungry. She examined carefully the long invisible coloured stream that the wind is made of. She selected the most interesting of its strands, and, nose-led, followed. In the corner of the iron-yard was a box of garbage. Among this she found something that answered fairly well for food; a bucket of water under a faucet offered a chance to quench her thirst.

The night was spent chiefly in prowling about and learning the main lines of the iron-yard. The next day she passed as before, sleeping in the sun. Thus the time wore on. Sometimes she found a good meal at the garbage-box, sometimes there was nothing. Once she found the big Black Tom there, but discreetly withdrew before he saw her. The water-bucket was usually at its place, or, failing that, there were some muddy little pools on the stone below. But the garbage-box was very unreliable. Once it left her for three days without food. She searched along the high fence, and seeing a small hole, crawled through that and found herself in the open street. This was a new world, but before she had ventured far, there was a noisy, rumbling rush – a large Dog came bounding, and Kitty had barely time to run back into the hole in the fence. She was dreadfully hungry, and glad to find some old potato-peelings, which gave a little respite from the hunger-pang. In the morning she did not sleep, but prowled for food. Some Sparrows chirruped in the yard. They were often there but now they were viewed with new eyes. The steady pressure of hunger had roused the wild hunter in the Kitten; those Sparrows were game – were food. She crouched instinctively and stalked from cover to cover, but the chirpers were alert and flew in time. Not once, but many times, she tried without result except to confirm the Sparrows in the list of things to be eaten if obtainable.

On the fifth day of ill luck the Slum Kitty ventured forth into the street, desperately bent on finding food. When far from the haven hole some small boys opened fire at her with pieces of brick. She ran in fear. A Dog joined in the chase, and Kitty's position grew perilous; but an old-fashioned iron fence round a house-front was there, and she slipped in between the rails as the Dog overtook her. A woman in a window above shouted at the Dog. Then the boys dropped a piece of cat-meat down to the unfortunate; and Kitty had the most delicious meal of her life. The stoop afforded a refuge. Under this she sat patiently till nightfall came with quiet, then sneaked back like a shadow to her old iron-yard.

Thus the days went by for two months. She grew in size and strength and in an intimate knowledge of the immediate neighbourhood. She made the acquaintance of Downey Street, where long rows of ash-cans were to be seen every morning. She formed her own ideas of their proprietors. The big house was to her, not a Roman Catholic mission, but a place whose garbage-tins abounded in choicest fish scrapings. She soon made the acquaintance of the meat-man, and joined in the shy fringe of Cats that formed the outer circle. She also met the Wharf Dog as well as two or three other horrors of the same class. She knew what to expect of them and how to avoid them; and she was happy in being the inventor of a new industry. Many thousand Cats have doubtless hung, in hope, about the tempting milk-cans that the early milk-man leaves on steps and window-ledges, and it was by the merest accident that Kitty found one with a broken lid, and so was taught to raise it and have a satisfying drink. Bottles, of course, were beyond her, but many a can has a misfit lid, and Kitty was very painstaking in her efforts to discover the loose-jointed ones. Finally she extended her range by exploration till she achieved the heart of the next block, and farther, till once more among the barrels and boxes of the yard behind the bird-man's cellar.

The old iron-yard never had been home, she had always felt like a stranger there; but here she had a sense of ownership, and at once resented the presence of another small Cat. She approached the newcomer with threatening air. The two had got as far as snarling and spitting when a bucket of water from an upper window drenched them both and effectually cooled their wrath. They fled, the newcomer over the wall, Slum Kitty under the very box where she had been born. This whole back region appealed to her strongly, and here again she took up her abode. The yard had no more garbage food than the other and no water at all, but it was frequented by Rats and a few Mice of the finest quality; these were occasionally secured, and afforded not only a palatable meal, but were the cause of her winning a friend.

IV

Kitty was now fully grown. She was a striking-looking Cat of the tiger type. Her marks were black on a very pale grey, and the four beauty-spots of white on nose, ears, and tail-tip lent a certain distinction. She was very expert at getting a living, and yet she had some days of starvation and failed in her ambition of catching a Sparrow. She was quite alone, but a new force was coming into her life.

She was lying in the sun one August day, when a large Black Cat came walking along the top of a wall in her direction. She recognized him at once by his torn ear. She slunk into her box and hid. He picked his way gingerly, bounded lightly to a shed that was at the end of the yard, and was crossing the roof when a Yellow Cat rose up. The Black Tom glared and growled, so did the Yellow Tom. Their tails lashed from side to side. Strong throats growled and yowled. They approached each other with ears laid back, with muscles a-tense.

'Yow-yow-ow!' said the Black One.

'Wow-w-w!' was the slightly deeper answer.

'Ya-wow-wow-wow!' said the Black One, edging up half an inch nearer.

'Yow-w-w!' was the Yellow answer, as the blond Cat rose to full height and stepped with vast dignity a whole inch forward. 'Yow-w!' and he went another inch, while his tail went swish, thump, from one side to the other.

'Ya-wow-yow-w!' screamed the Black in a rising tone, and he backed the eighth of an inch, as he marked the broad, unshrinking breast before him.

Windows opened all around, human voices were heard, but the Cat scene went on.

'Yow-yow-ow!' rumbled the Yellow Peril, his voice deepening as the other's rose. 'Yow!' and he advanced another step.

Now their noses were but three inches apart; they stood sidewise, both ready to clinch, but each waiting for the other. They glared for three minutes in silence and like statues, except that each tail-tip was twisting.

The Yellow began again. 'Yow-ow-ow!' in deep tone.

'Ya-a-a-a-a!' screamed the Black, with intent to strike terror by his yell; but he retreated one sixteenth of an inch. The Yellow walked up a long half-inch; their whiskers were mixing now; another advance, and their noses almost touched.

'Yo-w-w!' said Yellow, like a deep moan.

'Y-a-a-a-a-a!' screamed the Black, but he retreated a thirty-second of an inch, and the Yellow Warrior closed and clinched like a demon.

Oh, how they rolled and bit and tore, especially the Yellow One!

How they pitched and gripped and hugged, but especially the Yellow One!

Over and over, sometimes one on top, sometimes another, but mostly the Yellow One; and farther till they rolled off the roof, amid cheers from all the windows. They lost not a second in that fall to the junk-yard; they tore and clawed all the way down, but especially the Yellow One. And when they struck the ground, still fighting, the one on top was chiefly the Yellow One; and before they separated both had had as much as they wanted, especially the Black One! He scaled a wall and, bleeding and growling, disappeared, while the news was passed from window to window that Cayley's Nig had been licked at last by Orange Billy.

Either the Yellow Cat was a very clever seeker, or else Slum Kitty did not hide very hard; but he discovered her among the boxes, and she made no attempt to get away, probably because she had witnessed the fight. There is nothing like success in warfare to win the female heart, and thereafter the Yellow Tom and Kitty became very good friends, not sharing each other's lives or food – Cats do not do that way much – but recognizing each other as entitled to special friendly privileges.

V

September had gone. October's shortening days were on

when an event took place in the old cracker-box. If Orange Billy had come he would have seen five little Kittens curled up in the embrace of their mother, the little Slum Cat. It was a wonderful thing for her. She felt all the elation an animal mother can feel, all the delight, and she loved them and licked them with a tenderness that must have been a surprise to herself, had she had the power to think of such things.

She had added a joy to her joyless life, but she had also added a care and a heavy weight to her heavy load. All her strength was taken now to find food. The burden increased as the offspring grew up big enough to scramble about the boxes, which they did daily during her absence after they were six weeks old. That troubles go in flocks and luck in streaks, is well known in Slumland. Kitty had had three encounters with Dogs, and had been stoned by Malee's negro during a two days' starve. Then the tide turned. The very next morning she found a full milk-can without a lid, successfully robbed a barrow pensioner, and found a big fish-head, all within two hours. She had just returned with that perfect peace which comes with a full stomach, when she saw a little brown creature in her junk-yard. Hunting memories came back in strength; she didn't know what it was, but she had killed and eaten several Mice, and this was evidently a big Mouse with bob-tail and large ears. Kitty stalked it with elaborate but unnecessary caution; the little Rabbit simply sat up and looked faintly amused. He did not try to run, and Kitty sprang on him and bore him off. As she was not hungry, she carried him to the cracker-box and dropped him among the Kittens. He was not much hurt. He got over his fright, and since he could not get out of the box, he snuggled among the Kittens, and when they began to take their evening meal he very soon decided to join them. The old Cat was puzzled. The hunter instinct had been dominant, but absence of hunger had saved the Rabbit and given the maternal instinct a chance to appear. The result was that the Rabbit became a member of the family, and was thenceforth guarded and fed with the Kittens.

Two weeks went by. The Kittens romped much among the boxes during their mother's absence. The Rabbit could not get out of the box. Jap Malee, seeing the Kittens about the back yard, told the negro to shoot them. This he was doing one morning with a 22-calibre rifle. He had shot one after another and seen them drop from sight into the crannies of the lumber-pile, when the old Cat came running along the wall from the dock, carrying a small Wharf Rat. He had been ready to shoot her, too, but the sight of that Rat changed his plans: a rat-catching Cat was worthy to live. It happened to be the very first one she had ever caught, but it saved her life. She threaded the lumber-maze to the cracker-box and was probably puzzled to find that there were no Kittens to come at her call, and the Rabbit would not partake of the Rat. Pussy curled up to nurse the Rabbit, but she called from time to time to summon the Kittens. Guided by that call, the negro crawled quietly to the place, and peering down into the cracker-box, saw, to his intense surprise, that it contained the old Cat, a live Rabbit, and a dead Rat.

The mother Cat laid back her ears and snarled. The negro withdrew, but a minute later a board was dropped on the opening of the cracker-box, and the den with its tenants, dead and alive, was lifted into the bird-cellar.

'Say, boss, look a-hyar – hyar's where de little Rabbit got to wot we lost. Yo' sho t'ought Ah stoled him for de 'tater-bake.'

Kitty and Bunny were carefully put in a large wire cage and exhibited as a happy family till a few days later, when the Rabbit took sick and died.

Pussy had never been happy in the cage. She had enough to eat and drink, but she craved her freedom – would likely have gotten 'death or liberty' now, but that during the four days' captivity she had so cleaned and slicked her fur that her unusual colouring was seen, and Jap decided to keep her.

LIFE II

VI

Jap Malee was as disreputable a little Cockney bantam as ever sold cheap Canary-birds in a cellar. He was extremely poor, and the negro lived with him because the 'Henglishman' was willing to share bed and board, and otherwise admit a perfect equality that few Americans conceded. Jap was perfectly honest according to his lights, but he hadn't any lights; and it was well known that his chief revenue was derived from storing and restoring stolen Dogs and Cats. The half-dozen Canaries were mere blinds. Yet Jap believed in himself. 'Hi tell you, Sammy, me boy, you'll see me with 'orses of my own yet,' he would say, when some trifling success inflated his dirty little chest. He was not without ambition, in a weak, flabby, once-in-a-while way, and he sometimes wished to be known as a fancier. Indeed, he had once gone the wild length of offering a Cat for exhibition at the Knickerbocker High Society Cat and Pet Show, with three not over-clear objects: first, to gratify his ambition; second, to secure the exhibitor's free pass; and, third, 'well, you kneow, one 'as to kneow the valuable Cats, you kneow, when one goes a-catting.' But this was a society show, the exhibitor had to be introduced, and his miserable alleged half-Persian was scornfully rejected. The 'Lost and Found' columns of the papers were the only ones of interest to Jap, but he had noticed and saved a clipping about 'breeding for fur'. This was stuck on the wall of his den, and under its influence he set about what seemed a cruel experiment with the Slum Cat. First, he soaked her dirty fur with stuff to kill the two or three kinds of creepers she wore; and, when it had done its work, he washed her thoroughly in soap and warm water, in spite of her teeth, claws, and yowls. Kitty was savagely indignant, but a warm and happy glow spread over her as she dried off in a cage near the stove, and her fur began to fluff out with wonderful softness and whiteness. Jap and his assistant were much pleased with the result, and Kitty ought to have been. But this was preparatory: now for the experiment. 'Nothing is so good for growing fur as plenty of oily food and continued exposure to cold weather,' said the clipping. Winter was at hand, and Jap Malee put Kitty's cage out in the yard, protected only from the rain and the direct wind, and fed her with all the oil-cake and fish-heads she could eat. In a week a change began to show. She was rapidly getting fat and sleek – she had nothing to do but get fat and dress her fur. Her cage was kept clean, and nature responded to the chill weather and the oily food by making Kitty's coat thicker and glossier every day, so that by midwinter she was an unusually beautiful Cat in the fullest and finest of fur, with markings that were at least a rarity. Jap was much pleased with the result of the experiment, and as a very little success had a wonderful effect on him, he began to dream of the paths of glory. Why not send the Slum Cat to the show now coming on? The failure of the year before made him more careful as to details. ''T won't do, ye kneow, Sammy, to henter 'er as a tramp Cat, ye kneow,' he observed to his help; 'but it kin be arranged to suit the Knickerbockers. Nothink like a good noime, ye kneow. Ye see now it had orter be "Royal" somethink or other – nothink goes with the Knickerbockers like "Royal" anythink. Now "Royal Dick", or "Royal Sam", 'ow's that? But 'owld on; them's Tom names. Oi say, Sammy, wot's the noime of that island where ye wuz born?'

'Analostan Island, sah, was my native vicinity, sah.'

'Oi say, now, that's good, ye kneow. "Royal Analostan," by Jove! The onliest pedigreed "Royal Analostan" in the 'ole show, ye kneow. Ain't that foine?' and they mingled their cackles.

'But we'll ave to 'ave a pedigree, ye kneow.' So a very long fake pedigree on the recognized lines was prepared. One dark afternoon Sam, in a borrowed silk hat, delivered the Cat and the pedigree at the show door. The darkey did the honours. He had been a Sixth Avenue barber, and he could put on more pomp and lofty hauteur in five minutes than Jap Malee could have displayed in a lifetime, and this, doubtless, was one reason for the respectful reception awarded the Royal Analostan at the Cat Show.

Jap was very proud to be an exhibitor; but he had all a Cockney's reverence for the upper class, and when on the opening day he went to the door, he was overpowered to see the array of carriages and silk hats. The gate-man looked at him sharply, but passed him on his ticket, doubtless taking him for stable-boy to some exhibitor. The hall had velvet carpets before the long rows of cages. Jap, in his small cunning, was sneaking down the side rows, glancing at the Cats of all kinds, noting the blue ribbons and the reds, peering about but not daring to ask for his own exhibit, only trembling to think what the gorgeous gathering of fashion would say if they discovered the trick he was playing on them. He had passed all around the outer aisles and seen many prize-winners, but no sign of Slum Kitty. The inner aisles were more crowded. He picked his way down them, but still no Kitty, and he decided that it was a mistake; the judges had rejected the Cat later. Never mind; he had his exhibitor's ticket, and now knew where several valuable Persians and Angoras were to be found.

In the middle of the centre aisle were the high-class Cats. A great throng was there. The passage was roped, and two policemen were in place to keep the crowd moving. Jap wriggled in among them; he was too short to see over, and though the richly gowned folks shrunk from his shabby old clothes, he could not get near; but he gathered from the remarks that the gem of the show was there.

'Oh, isn't she a beauty!' said one tall woman.

'What distinction!' was the reply.

'One cannot mistake the air that comes only from ages of the most refined surroundings.'

'How I should like to own that superb creature!'

'Such dignity – such repose!'

'She has an authentic pedigree nearly back to the Pharaohs, I hear'; and poor, dirty little Jap marvelled at his own cheek in sending his Slum Cat into such company.

'Excuse me, madame.' The director of the show now appeared, edging his way through the crowd. 'The artist of the "Sporting Element" is here, under orders to sketch the "pearl of the show" for immediate use. May I ask you to stand a little aside? That's it; thank you.'

'Oh, Mr Director, cannot you persuade him to sell that beautiful creature?'

'Hm, I don't know,' was the reply. 'I understand he is a man of ample means and not at all approachable; but I'll try, I'll try, madame. He was quite unwilling to exhibit his treasure at all, so I understand from his butler. Here, you, keep out of the way,' growled the director, as the shabby little man eagerly pushed between the artist and the blue-blooded Cat. But the disreputable one wanted to know where valuable Cats were to be found. He came near enough to get a glimpse of the cage, and there read a placard which announced that 'The blue ribbon and *gold medal* of the Knickerbocker High Society Cat and Pet Show' had been awarded to the 'thoroughbred, pedigreed Royal Analostan, imported and exhibited by J. Malee, Esq., the well-known fancier. (Not for sale.)' Jap caught his breath and stared again. Yes, surely; there, high in a gilded cage, on velvet cushions, with four policemen for guards, her fur bright black and pale grey, her bluish eyes slightly closed, was his Slum Kitty, looking the picture of a Cat bored to death with a lot of fuss that she likes as little as she understands it.

VII

Jap Malee lingered around that cage, taking in the remarks, for hours – drinking a draught of glory such as he had never known in life before and rarely glimpsed in his dreams. But he saw that it would be wise for him to remain unknown; his 'butler' must do all the business.

It was Slum Kitty who made that show a success. Each day her value went up in her owner's eyes. He did not know what prices had been given for Cats, and thought that he was touching a record pitch when his 'butler' gave the director authority to sell the Analostan for one hundred dollars.

This is how it came about that the Slum Cat found herself transferred from the show to a Fifth Avenue mansion. She evinced a most unaccountable wildness at first. Her objection to petting, however, was explained on the ground of her aristocratic dislike of familiarity. Her retreat from the Lap-dog on to the centre of the dinner-table was understood to express a deep-rooted though mistaken idea of avoiding a defiling touch. Her assaults on a pet Canary were condoned for the reason that in her native Orient she had been used to despotic example. The patrician way in which she would get the cover off a milk-can was especially applauded. Her dislike of her silk-lined basket, and her frequent dashes against the plate-glass windows, were easily understood: the basket was too plain, and plate-glass was not used in her royal home. Her spotting of the carpet evidenced her Eastern modes of thought. The failure of her several attempts to catch Sparrows in the high-walled back yard was new proof of the royal impotency of her bringing up; while her frequent wallowings in the garbage-can were understood to be the manifestation of a little pardonable high-born eccentricity. She was fed and pampered, shown and praised; but she was not happy. Kitty was homesick! She clawed at that blue ribbon round her neck till she got it off; she jumped against the plate-glass because that seemed the road to outside; she avoided people and Dogs because they had always proved hostile and cruel; and she would sit and gaze on the roofs and back yards at the other side of the window, wishing she could be among them for a change.

But she was strictly watched, was never allowed outside – so that all the happy garbage-can moments occurred while these receptacles of joy were indoors. One night in March, however, as they were set out a-row for the early scavenger, the Royal Analostan saw her chance, slipped out of the door, and was lost to view.

Of course there was a grand stir; but Pussy neither knew nor cared anything about that – her one thought was to go home. It may have been chance that took her back in the direction of Gramercy Grange Hill, but she did arrive there after sundry small adventures. And now what? She was not at home, and she had cut off her living. She was beginning to be hungry, and yet she had a peculiar sense of happiness. She cowered in a front garden for some time. A raw east wind had been rising, and now it came to her with a particularly friendly message; man would have called it an unpleasant smell of docks, but to Pussy it was welcome tidings from home. She trotted down the long street due east, threading the rails of front gardens, stopping like a statue for an instant, or crossing the street in search of the darkest side, and came at length to the docks and to the water. But the place was strange. She could go north or south. Something turned her southward; and, dodging among docks and Dogs, carts and Cats, crooked arms of the bay and straight board fences, she got, in an hour or two, among familiar scenes and smells; and, before the sun came up, she had crawled back weary and foot-sore through the same old hole in the same old fence and over a wall to her junk-yard back of the bird-cellar – yes, back into the very cracker-box where she was born.

Oh, if the Fifth Avenue family could only have seen her in her native Orient!

After a long rest she came quietly down from the cracker-box towards the steps leading to the cellar, engaged in her old-time pursuit of seeking for eatables. The door opened, and there stood the negro. He shouted to the bird-man inside:

'Say, boss, com hyar. Ef dere ain't dat dar Royal Ankalostan am comed back!'

Jap came in time to see the Cat jumping the wall. They called loudly and in the most seductive, wheedling tones: 'Pussy, Pussy, poor Pussy! Come, Pussy!' But Pussy was not prepossessed in their favour, and disappeared to forage in her old-time haunts.

The Royal Analostan had been a windfall for Jap – had been the means of adding many comforts to cellar and several prisoners to the cages. It was now of the utmost importance to recapture her majesty. Stale meat-offal and other infallible lures were put out till Pussy, urged by the re-established hunger-pinch, crept up to a large fish-head in a box-trap; the negro, in watching, pulled the string that dropped the lid, and, a minute later, the Analostan was once more among the prisoners in the cellar. Meanwhile Jap had been watching the 'Lost and Found' column. There it was, '$25 reward' etc. That night Mr Malee's butler called at the Fifth Avenue mansion with the missing cat. 'Mr Malee's compliments, sah. De Royal Analostan had recurred in her recent proprietor's vicinity and residence, sah. Mr Malee had pleasure in recuperating the Royal Analostan, sah.' Of course Mr Malee could not be rewarded, but the butler was open to any offer, and plainly showed that he expected the promised reward and something more.

Kitty was guarded very carefully after that; but so far from being disgusted with the old life of starving, and glad of her ease, she became wilder and more dissatisfied.

VIII

The spring was doing its New York best. The dirty little English Sparrows were tumbling over each other in their gutter brawls, Cats yowled all night in the areas, and the Fifth Avenue family were thinking of their country residence. They packed up, closed house, and moved off to their summer home, some fifty miles away, and Pussy, in a basket, went with them.

'Just what she needed: a change of air and scene to wean her away from her former owners and make her happy.'

The basket was lifted into a Rumble-shaker. New sounds

and passing smells were entered and left. A turn in the course was made. Then a roaring of many feet, more swinging of the basket; a short pause, another change of direction, then some clicks, some bangs, a long shrill whistle, and door-bells of a very big front door; a rumbling, a whizzing, an unpleasant smell, a hideous smell, a growing horrible, hateful choking smell, a deadly, griping, poisonous stench, with roaring that drowned poor Kitty's yowls, and just as it neared the point where endurance ceased, there was relief. She heard clicks and clacks. There was light; there was air. Then a man's voice called, 'All out for 125th Street,' though of course to Kitty it was a mere human bellow. The roaring almost ceased – did cease. Later the rackety-bang was renewed with plenty of sounds and shakes, though not the poisonous gas; a long, hollow, booming roar with a pleasant dock smell was quickly passed, and then there was a succession of jolts, roars, jars, stops, clicks, clacks, smells, jumps, shakes, more smells, more shakes – big shakes, little shakes – gases, smokes, screeches, door-bells, tremblings, roars, thunders, and some new smells, raps, taps, heavings, rumblings, and more smells, but all without any of the feel that the direction is changed. When at last it stopped, the sun came twinkling through the basket-lid. The Royal Cat was lifted into a Rumble-shaker of the old familiar style, and, swerving aside from their past course, very soon the noises of its wheels were grittings and rattlings; a new and horrible sound was added – the barking of Dogs, big and little and dreadfully close. The basket was lifted, and Slum Kitty had reached her country home.

Every one was officiously kind. They wanted to please the Royal Cat, but somehow none of them did, except, possibly, the big, fat cook that Kitty discovered on wandering into the kitchen. This unctuous person smelt more like a slum than anything she had met for months, and the Royal Analostan was proportionately attracted. The cook, when she learned that fears were entertained about the Cat staying, said: 'Shure, she'd 'tind to thot; wanst a Cat licks her futs, shure she's at home.' So she deftly caught the unapproachable royalty in her apron, and committed the horrible sacrilege of greasing the soles of her feet with pot-grease. Of course Kitty resented it – she resented everything in the place; but on being set down she began to dress her paws and found evident satisfaction in that grease. She licked all four feet for an hour, and the cook triumphantly announced that now 'shure she'd be apt to shtay'. And stay she did, but she showed a most surprising and disgusting preference for the kitchen, the cook, and the garbage-pail.

The family, though distressed by these distinguished peculiarities, were glad to see the Royal Analostan more contented and approachable. They gave her more liberty after a week or two. They guarded her from every menace. The Dogs were taught to respect her. No man or boy about the place would have dreamed of throwing a stone at the famous pedigreed Cat. She had all the food she wanted, but still she was not happy. She was hankering for many things, she scarcely knew what. She had everything – yes, but she wanted something else. Plenty to eat and drink – yes, but milk does not taste the same when you can go and drink all you want from a saucer; it has to be stolen out of a tin pail when you are belly-pinched with hunger and thirst, or it does not have the tang – it isn't milk.

Yes, there *was* a junk-yard back of the house and beside it and around it too, a big one, but it was everywhere poisoned and polluted with roses. The very Horses and Dogs had the wrong smells; the whole country round was a repellent desert of lifeless, disgusting gardens and hay-fields, without a single tenement or smoke-stack in sight.

How she did hate it all! There was only one sweet-smelling shrub in the whole horrible place, and that was in a neglected corner. She did enjoy nipping that and rolling in the leaves; it was a bright spot in the grounds; but the only one, for she had not found a rotten fish-head nor seen a genuine garbage-can since she came, and altogether it was the most unlovely, unattractive, unsmellable spot she had ever known. She would surely have gone that first night had she had the liberty. The liberty was weeks in coming, and, meanwhile, her affinity with the cook had developed as a bond to keep her; but one day after a summer of discontent a succession of things happened to stir anew the slum instinct of the royal prisoner.

A great bundle of stuff from the docks had reached the country mansion. What it contained was of little moment, but it was rich with a score of the most piquant and winsome of dock and slum smells. The chords of memory surely dwell in the nose, and Pussy's past was conjured up with dangerous force. Next day the cook 'left' through some trouble over this very bundle. It was the cutting of cables, and that evening the youngest boy of the house, a horrid little American with no proper appreciation of royalty, was tying a tin to the blue-blooded one's tail, doubtless in furtherance of some altruistic project, when Pussy resented the liberty with a paw that wore five big fish-hooks for the occasion. The howl of downtrodden America roused America's mother. The deft and womanly blow that she aimed with her book was miraculously avoided, and Pussy took flight, upstairs, of course. A hunted Rat runs downstairs, a hunted Dog goes on the level, a hunted Cat runs up. She hid in the garret, baffled discovery, and waited till night came. Then, gliding downstairs, she tried each screen-door in turn, till she found one unlatched, and escaped into the black August night. Pitch-black to man's eyes, it was simply grey to her, and she glided through the disgusting shrubbery and flower-beds, took a final nip at that one little bush that had been an attractive spot in the garden, and boldly took her back track of the spring.

How could she take a back track that she never saw? There is in all animals some sense of direction. It is very low in man and very high in Horses, but Cats have a large gift, and this mysterious guide took her westward, not clearly and definitely, but with a general impulse that was made definite simply because the road was easy to travel. In an hour she had covered two miles and reached the Hudson River. Her nose had told her many times that the course was true. Smell after smell came back, just as a man after walking a mile in a strange street may not recall a single feature, but will remember, on seeing it again, 'Why, yes, I saw that before.' So Kitty's main guide was the sense of direction, but it was her nose that kept reassuring her, 'Yes, now you are right – we passed this place last spring.'

At the river was the railroad. She could not go on the water; she must go north or south. This was a case where her sense of direction was clear; it said, 'Go south', and Kitty trotted down the foot-path between the iron rails and the fence.

LIFE III

IX

Cats can go very fast up a tree or over a wall, but when it comes to the long steady trot that reels off mile after mile, hour after hour, it is not the cat-hop, but the dog-trot, that counts. Although the travelling was good and the path direct, an hour had gone before two more miles were put between her and the Hades of roses. She was tired and a little foot-sore. She was thinking of rest when a Dog came running to the fence near by, and broke out into such a horrible barking close to her ear that Pussy leaped in terror. She ran as hard as she could down the path, at the same time watching to see if the Dog should succeed in passing the fence. No, not yet! but he ran close by it, growling horribly, while Pussy skipped along on the safe side. The barking of the Dog grew into a low rumble – a louder rumble and roaring – a terrifying thunder. A light shone. Kitty glanced back to see, not the Dog, but a huge Black Thing with a blazing red eye coming on, yowling and spitting like a yard full of Cats. She put forth all her powers to run, made such time as she had never made before, but dared not leap the fence. She was running like a Dog, was flying, but all in vain; the monstrous pursuer overtook her, but missed her in the darkness, and hurried past to be lost in the night, while Kitty crouched gasping for breath, half a mile nearer home since that Dog began to bark.

This was her first encounter with the strange monster, strange to her eyes only; her nose seemed to know him and told her this was another landmark on the home trail. But Pussy lost much of her fear of his kind. She learned that they were very stupid and could not find her if she slipped quietly under a fence and lay still. Before morning she had encountered several of them, but escaped unharmed from all.

About sunrise she reached a nice little slum on her home trail, and was lucky enough to find several unsterilized eatables in an ash-heap. She spent the day around a stable where were two Dogs and a number of small boys, that between them came near ending her career. It was so very like home; but she had no idea of staying there. She was driven by the old craving, and next evening set out as before. She had seen the one-eyed Thunder-rollers all day going by, and was getting used to them, so travelled steadily all that night. The next day was spent in a barn where she caught a Mouse, and the next night was like the last, except that a Dog she encountered drove her backwards on her trail for a long way. Several times she was misled by angling roads, and wandered far astray, but in time she wandered back again to her general southward course. The days were passed in skulking under barns and hiding from Dogs and small boys, and the nights in limping along the track, for she was getting foot-sore; but on she went, mile after mile, southward, ever southward – Dogs, boys, Roarers, hunger – Dogs, boys, Roarers, hunger – yet on and onward still she went, and her nose from time to time cheered her by confidently reporting, 'There surely is a smell we passed last spring.'

X

So a week went by, and Pussy, dirty, ribbonless, foot-sore, and weary, arrived at the Harlem Bridge. Though it was enveloped in delicious smells, she did not like the look of that bridge. For half the night she wandered up and down the shore without discovering any other means of going south, excepting some other bridges, or anything of interest except that here the men were as dangerous as the boys. Somehow she had to come back to it; not only its smells were familiar, but from time to time, when a One-eye ran over it, there was that peculiar rumbling roar that was a sensation in the springtime trip. The calm of the late night was abroad when she leaped to the timber stringer and glided out over the water. She had got less than a third of the way across when a thundering One-eye came roaring at her from the opposite end. She was much frightened, but knowing their stupidity and blindness, she dropped to a low side beam and there crouched in hiding. Of course the stupid Monster missed her and passed on, and all would have been well, but it turned back, or another just like it came suddenly spitting behind her. Pussy leaped to the long track and made for the home shore. She might have got there had not a third of the Red-eyed Terrors come screeching at her from that side. She was running her hardest, but was caught between two foes. There was nothing for it but a desperate leap from the timbers into – she didn't know what. Down, down, down – plop, splash, plunge into the deep water, not cold, for it was August, but oh, so horrible! She spluttered and coughed when she came to the top, glanced around to see if the Monsters were swimming after her, and struck out for shore. She had never learned to swim, and yet she swam, for the simple reason that a Cat's position and actions in swimming are the same as her position and actions in walking. She had fallen into a place she did not like; naturally she tried to *walk* out, and the result was that she swam ashore. Which shore? The home-love never fails: the south side was the only shore for her, the one nearest home. She scrambled out all dripping wet, up the muddy bank and through coal-piles and dust-heaps, looking as black, dirty, and unroyal as it was possible for a Cat to look.

Once the shock was over, the Royal-pedigreed Slummer began to feel better for the plunge. A genial glow without from the bath, a genial sense of triumph within, for had she not outwitted three of the big Terrors?

Her nose, her memory, and her instinct of direction inclined her to get on the track again; but the place was infested with those Thunder-rollers, and prudence led her to turn aside and follow the river-bank with its musky home-reminders; and thus she was spared the unspeakable horrors of the tunnel.

She was over three days learning the manifold dangers and complexities of the East River docks. Once she got by mistake on a ferry-boat and was carried over to Long Island; but she took an early boat back. At length on the third night she reached familiar ground, the place she had passed the night of her first escape. From that her course was sure and rapid. She knew just where she was going and how to get there. She knew even the more prominent features in the Dog-scape now. She went faster, felt happier. In a little while surely she would be curled up in her native Orient – the old junk-yard. Another turn, and the block was in sight.

But – what! It was gone! Kitty couldn't believe her eyes; but she must, for the sun was not yet up. There where once had stood or leaned or slouched or straggled the houses of the block, was a great broken wilderness of stone, lumber, and holes in the ground.

Kitty walked all around it. She knew by the bearings and by the local colour of the pavement that she was in her home, that there had lived the bird-man, and there was the old junk-yard; but all were gone, completely gone, taking their familiar odours with them, and Pussy turned sick at heart in the utter hopelessness of the case. Her place-love was her master-mood. She had given up all to come to a home that no longer existed, and for once her sturdy little heart was cast down. She wandered over the silent heaps of rubbish and found neither consolation nor eatables. The ruin had taken in several of the blocks and reached back from the water. It was not a fire; Kitty had seen one of those things. This looked more like the work of a flock of the Red-eyed Monsters. Pussy knew nothing of the great bridge that was to rise from this very spot.

When the sun came up she sought for cover. An adjoining block still stood with little change, and the Royal Analostan retired to that. She knew some of its trails; but once there, was unpleasantly surprised to find the place swarming with Cats that, like herself, were driven from their old grounds, and when the garbage-cans came out there were several Slummers at each. It meant a famine in the land, and Pussy, after standing it a few days, was reduced to seeking her other home on Fifth Avenue. She got there to find it shut up and deserted. She waited about for a day; had an unpleasant experience with a big man in a blue coat, and next night returned to the crowded slum.

September and October wore away. Many of the Cats died of starvation or were too weak to escape their natural enemies. But Kitty, young and strong, still lived.

Great changes had come over the ruined blocks. Though silent on the night when she first saw them, they were crowded with noisy workmen all day. A tall building, well advanced on her arrival, was completed at the end of October, and Slum Kitty, driven by hunger, went sneaking up to a pail that a negro had set outside. The pail, unfortunately, was not for garbage; it was a new thing in that region: a scrubbing-pail. A sad disappointment, but it had a sense of comfort – there were traces of a familiar touch on the handle. While she was studying it, the negro elevator-boy came out again. In spite of his blue clothes, his odorous person confirmed the good impression of the handle. Kitty had retreated across the street. He gazed at her.

'Sho ef dat don't look like de Royal Ankalostan! Hyar, Pussy, Pussy, Pu-s-s-s-y! Co-o-o-m-e, Pu-u-s-s-sy, hyar! I 'spec's she's sho hungry.'

Hungry! She hadn't had a real meal for months. The negro went into the building and reappeared with a portion of his own lunch.

'Hyar, Pussy, Puss, Puss, Puss!' It seemed very good, but Pussy had her doubts of the man. At length he laid the meat on the pavement, and went back to the door. Slum Kitty came forward very warily; sniffed at the meat, seized it, and fled like a little Tigress to eat her prize in peace.

LIFE IV

XI

This was the beginning of a new era. Pussy came to the door of the building now whenever pinched by hunger, and the good feeling for the negro grew. She had never understood that man before. He had always seemed hostile. Now he was her friend, the only one she had.

One week she had a streak of luck. Seven good meals on seven successive days; and right on the top of the last meal she found a juicy dead Rat, the genuine thing, a perfect windfall. She had never killed a full-grown Rat in all her lives, but seized the prize and ran off to hide it for future use. She was crossing the street in front of the new building when an old enemy appeared – the Wharf Dog – and Kitty retreated, naturally enough, to the door where she had a friend. Just as she neared it, he opened the door for a well-dressed man to come out, and both saw the Cat with her prize.

'Hello! Look at that for a Cat!'

'Yes, sah,' answered the negro. 'Dat's ma Cat, sah; she's a terror on Rats, sah! hez 'em about cleaned up, sah; dat's why she's so thin.'

'Well, don't let her starve,' said the man with the air of the landlord. 'Can't you feed her?'

'De liver meat-man comes reg'lar, sah; quatah dollar a

week, sah,' said the negro, fully realizing that he was entitled to the extra fifteen cents for 'the idea'.

'That's all right. I'll stand it.'

XII

'M-e-a-t! M-e-a-t!' is heard the magnetic, cat-conjuring cry of the old liver-man, as his barrow is pushed up the glorified Scrimper's Alley, and Cats come crowding, as of yore, to receive their due.

There are Cats black, white, yellow, and grey to be remembered, and, above all, there are owners to be remembered. As the barrow rounds the corner near the new building it makes a newly scheduled stop.

'Hyar, you, get out o' the road, you common trash,' cries the liver-man, and he waves his wand to make way for the little grey Cat with blue eyes and white nose. She receives an unusually large portion, for Sam is wisely dividing the returns evenly; and Slum Kitty retreats with her 'daily' into shelter of the great building, to which she is regularly attached. She has entered into her fourth life with prospects of happiness never before dreamed of. Everything was against her at first; now everything seems to be coming her way. It is very doubtful that her mind was broadened by travel, but she knew what she wanted and she got it. She has achieved her long-time great ambition by catching, not *a* Sparrow, but two of them, while they were clinched in mortal combat in the gutter.

There is no reason to suppose that she ever caught another Rat; but the negro secures a dead one when he can, for purposes of exhibition, lest her pension be imperilled. The dead one is left in the hall till the proprietor comes; then it is apologetically swept away. 'Well, drat dat

Cat, sah; dat Royal Ankalostan blood, sah, is terrors on Rats.'

She has had several broods since. The negro thinks the Yellow Tom is the father of some of them, and no doubt the negro is right.

He has sold her a number of times with a perfectly clear conscience, knowing quite well that it is only a question of a few days before the Royal Analostan comes back again. Doubtless he is saving the money for some honourable ambition. She has learned to tolerate the elevator, and even to ride up and down on it. The negro stoutly maintains that once, when she heard the meat-man, while she was on the top floor, she managed to press the button that called the elevator to take her down.

She is sleek and beautiful again. She is not only one of the four hundred that form the inner circle about the liver-barrow, but she is recognized as the star pensioner among them. The liver-man is positively respectful. Not even the cream-and-chicken fed Cat of the pawn-broker's wife has such a position as the Royal Analostan. But in spite of her prosperity, her social position, her royal name and fake pedigree, the greatest pleasure of her life is to slip out and go a-slumming in the gloaming, for now, as in her previous lives, she is at heart, and likely to be, nothing but a dirty little Slum Cat.

Silverspot

The Story of a Crow

I

How many of us have ever got to know a wild animal? I do not mean merely to meet with one once or twice, or to have one in a cage, but to really know it for a long time while it is wild, and to get an insight into its life and history. The trouble usually is to know one creature from his fellow. One fox or crow is so much like another that we cannot be sure that it really is the same next time we meet. But once in awhile there arises an animal who is stronger or wiser than his fellow, who becomes a great leader, who is, as we would say, a genius, and if he is bigger, or has some mark by which men can know him, he soon becomes famous in his country, and shows us that the life of a wild animal may be far more interesting and exciting than that of many human beings.

Of this class were Courtrand, the bob-tailed wolf that terrorized the whole city of Paris for about ten years in the beginning of the fourteenth century; Clubfoot, the lame grizzly bear that left such a terrific record in the San Joaquin Valley of California; Lobo, the king-wolf of New Mexico, that killed a cow every day for five years, and the Soehnee panther that in less than two years killed nearly three hundred human beings – and such also was Silverspot, whose history, so far as I could learn it, I shall now briefly tell.

Silverspot was simply a wise old crow; his name was given because of the silvery white spot that was like a nickel, stuck on his right side, between the eye and the bill, and it was owing to this spot that I was able to know him from the other crows, and put together the parts of his history that came to my knowledge.

Crows are, as you must know, our most intelligent birds – 'Wise as an old crow' did not become a saying without good reason. Crows know the value of organization, and are as well drilled as soldiers – very much better than some soldiers, in fact, for crows are always on duty, always at war, and always dependent on each other for life and safety. Their leaders not only are the oldest and wisest of the band, but also the strongest and bravest, for they must be ready at any time with sheer force to put down an upstart or a rebel. The rank and file are the youngsters and the crows without special gifts.

Old Silverspot was the leader of a large band of crows that made their headquarters near Toronto, Canada, in Castle Frank, which is a pine-clad hill on the northeast edge of the city. This band numbered about two hundred, and for reasons that I never understood did not increase. In mild winters they stayed along the Niagara River; in cold winters they went much farther south. But each year in the last week of February Old Silverspot would muster his followers and boldly cross the forty miles of open water that lies between Toronto and Niagara; not, however, in a straight line would he go, but always in a curve to the west, whereby he kept in sight of the familiar landmark of Dundas Mountain, until the pine-clad hill itself came in view. Each year he came with his troop, and for about six weeks took up his abode on the hill. Each morning thereafter the crows set out in three bands to forage. One band went southeast to Ashbridge's Bay. One went north up the Don, and one, the largest, went northwestward up the ravine. The last Silverspot led in person. Who led the others I never found out.

On calm mornings they flew high and straight away. But when it was windy the band flew low, and followed the ravine for shelter. My windows overlooked the ravine, and it was thus that in 1885 I first noticed this old crow. I was a new-comer in the neighbourhood, but an old resident said to me then 'that there old crow has been a-flying up and down this ravine for more than twenty years'. My chances to watch were in the ravine, and Silverspot doggedly clinging to the old route, though now it was edged with houses and spanned by bridges, became a very familiar acquaintance. Twice each day in March and part of April, then again in the late summer and the fall, he passed and repassed, and gave me chances to see his movements, and hear his orders to his bands, and so, little by little, opened my eyes to the fact that the crows, though a little people, are of great wit, a race of birds with a language and a social system that is wonderfully human in many of its chief points, and in some is better carried out than our own.

One windy day I stood on the high bridge across the ravine, as the old crow, heading his long, straggling troop, came flying down homeward. Half a mile away I could hear the contented *'All's well, come right along!'* as we should

say, or as he put it, and as also his lieutenant echoed it at the rear of the band. They were flying very low to be out of the wind, and would have to rise a little to clear the bridge on which I was. Silverspot saw me standing there, and as I was closely watching him he didn't like it. He checked his flight and called out, '*Be on your guard*', or

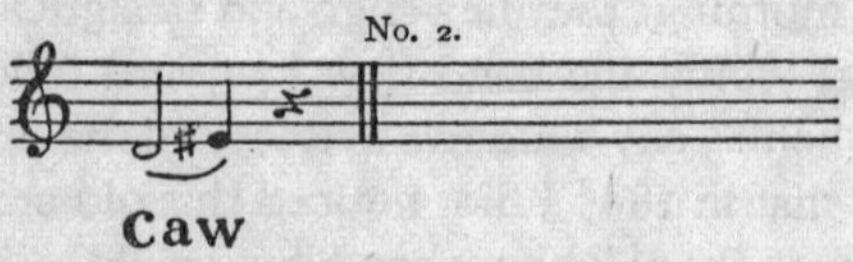

and rose much higher in the air. Then seeing that I was not armed he flew over my head about twenty feet, and his followers in turn did the same, dipping again to the old level when past the bridge.

Next day I was at the same place, and as the crows came near I raised my walking stick and pointed it at them. The old fellow at once cried out '*Danger*', and rose fifty feet

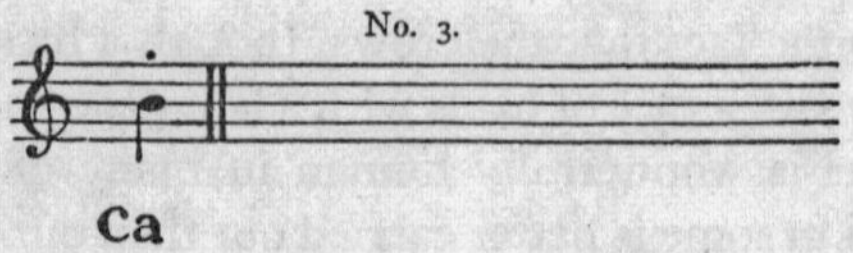

higher than before. Seeing that it was not a gun, he ventured to fly over. But on the third day I took with me a gun, and at once he cried out, '*Great danger – a gun.*' His lieu-

tenant repeated the cry, and every crow in the troop began to tower and scatter from the rest, till they were far above gun shot, and so passed safely over, coming down again to the shelter of the valley when well beyond reach. Another time, as the long, straggling troop came down the valley, a red-tailed hawk alighted on a tree close by their intended route. The leader cried out, *'Hawk, hawk'*, and stayed his

flight, as did each crow on nearing him, until all were massed in a solid body. Then, no longer fearing the hawk, they passed on. But a quarter of a mile farther on a man with a gun appeared below, and the cry, *'Great danger – a gun, a gun; scatter for your lives'*, at once caused them to

scatter widely and tower till far beyond range. Many others of his words of command I learned in the course of my long acquaintance, and found that sometimes a very little difference in the sound makes a very great difference in meaning. Thus while No. 5 means hawk, or any large, dangerous bird, this means *'wheel around'*, evidently a combination of

No. 5, whose root idea is danger, and of No. 4, whose root idea is retreat, and this again is a mere '*good day*', to a far

away comrade. This is usually addressed to the ranks and means '*attention*'.

Early in April there began to be great doings among the crows. Some new cause of excitement seemed to have come on them. They spent half the day among the pines, instead of foraging from dawn till dark. Pairs and trios might be seen chasing each other, and from time to time they showed off in various feats of flight. A favourite sport was to dart down suddenly from a great height towards some perching crow, and just before touching it to turn at a hairbreadth and rebound in the air so fast that the wings of the swooper whirred with a sound like distant thunder. Sometimes one crow would lower his head, raise every feather, and coming close to another would gurgle out a long note like

What did it all mean? I soon learned. They were making love and pairing off. The males were showing off their wing powers and their voices to the lady crows. And they must have been highly appreciated, for by the middle of April all had mated and had scattered over the country for their honeymoon, leaving the sombre old pines of Castle Frank deserted and silent.

II

The Sugar Loaf hill stands alone in the Don Valley. It is still covered with woods that join with those of Castle Frank, a quarter of a mile off. In the woods, between the two hills, is a pine-tree in whose top is a deserted hawk's nest. Every Toronto school-boy knows the nest, and, excepting that I had once shot a black squirrel on its edge, no one had ever seen a sign of life about it. There it was year after year, ragged and old, and falling to pieces. Yet, strange to tell, in all that time it never did drop to pieces, like other old nests.

One morning in May I was out at grey dawn, and stealing gently through the woods, whose dead leaves were so wet that no rustle was made. I chanced to pass under the old nest, and was surprised to see a black tail sticking over the edge. I struck the tree a smart blow, off flew a crow, and the secret was out. I had long suspected that a pair of crows nested each year about the pines, but now I realized that it was Silverspot and his wife. The old nest was theirs, and they were too wise to give it an air of spring-cleaning and housekeeping each year. Here they had nested for long, though guns in the hands of men and boys hungry to shoot crows were carried under their home every day. I never surprised the old fellow again, though I several times saw him through my telescope.

One day while watching I saw a crow crossing the Don Valley with something white in his beak. He flew to the mouth of the Rosedale Brook, then took a short flight to the Beaver Elm. There he dropped the white object, and looking about gave me a chance to recognize my old friend Silverspot. After a minute he picked up the white thing – a shell – and walked over past the spring, and here, among the docks and the skunk-cabbages, he unearthed a pile of shells and other white, shiny things. He spread them out in the sun, turned them over, lifted them one by one in his beak, dropped them, nestled on them as though they were eggs, toyed with them and gloated over them like a miser. This was his hobby, his weakness. He could not have explained *why* he enjoyed them, any more than a boy can explain why he collects postage-stamps, or a girl why she prefers pearls to rubies; but his pleasure in them was very real, and after half an hour he covered them all, including the new one, with earth and leaves, and flew off. I went at once to the spot and examined the hoard; there was about a hatful in all, chiefly white pebbles, clam-shells, and some bits of tin, but there was also the handle of a china cup, which must have been the gem of the collection. That was the last time I saw them. Silverspot knew that I had found his treasures, and he removed them at once; where I never knew.

During the space that I watched him so closely he had many little adventures and escapes. He was once severely handled by a sparrowhawk, and often he was chased and worried by kingbirds. Not that these did him much harm, but they were such noisy pests that he avoided their company as quickly as possible, just as a grown man avoids a conflict with a noisy and impudent small boy. He had some cruel tricks, too. He had a way of going the round of the small birds' nests each morning to eat the new laid eggs, as regularly as a doctor visiting his patients. But we must not judge him for that, as it is just what we ourselves do to the hens in the barnyard.

His quickness of wit was often shown. One day I saw him flying down the ravine with a large piece of bread in his bill. The stream below him was at this time being bricked over as a sewer. There was one part of two hundred yards quite finished, and, as he flew over the open water just above this, the bread fell from his bill, and was swept by the current out of sight into the tunnel. He flew down and peered vainly into the dark cavern, then, acting upon a happy thought, he flew to the downstream end of the tunnel, and awaiting the reappearance of the floating bread, as it was swept onward by the current, he seized and bore it off in triumph.

Silverspot was a crow of the world. He was truly a successful crow. He lived in a region that, though full of dangers, abounded with food. In the old, unrepaired nest he raised a brood each year with his wife, whom, by the way, I never could distinguish, and when the crows again gathered together he was their acknowledged chief.

The reassembling takes place about the end of June – the young crows with their bob-tails, soft wings, and falsetto voices are brought by their parents, whom they nearly equal in size, and introduced to society at the old pine woods, a woods that is at once their fortress and college. Here they find security in numbers and in lofty yet sheltered perches, and here they begin their schooling and are taught all the secrets of success in crow life, and in crow life the least failure does not simply mean begin again. It means *death*.

The first week or two after their arrival is spent by the young ones in getting acquainted, for each crow must know personally all the others in the band. Their parents meanwhile have time to rest a little after the work of raising them, for now the youngsters are able to feed themselves and roost on a branch in a row, just like big folks.

In a week or two the moulting season comes. At this time the old crows are usually irritable and nervous, but it does not stop them from beginning to drill the youngsters; who, of course, do not much enjoy the punishment and nagging they get so soon after they have been mamma's own darlings. But it is all for their good, as the old lady said when she skinned the eels, and old Silverspot is an excellent teacher. Sometimes he seems to make a speech to them. What he says I cannot guess, but, judging by the way they receive it, it must be extremely witty. Each morning there is a company drill, for the young ones naturally drop into two or three squads according to their age and strength. The rest of the day they forage with their parents.

When at length September comes we find a great change. The rabble of silly little crows have begun to learn sense. The delicate blue iris of their eyes, the sign of a fool-crow, has given place to the dark brown eye of the old stager. They know their drill now and have learned sentry duty. They have been taught guns and traps and taken a special course in wire-worms and greencorn. They know that a fat old farmer's wife is much less dangerous, though so much larger, than her fifteen-year-old son, and they can tell the boy from his sister. They know that an umbrella is not a gun, and they can count up to six, which is fair for young crows, though Silverspot can go up nearly to thirty. They know the smell of gun-powder and the south side of a hemlock-tree, and begin to plume themselves upon being crows of the world. They always fold their wings three times after alighting, to be sure that it is neatly done. They know how to worry a fox into giving up half his dinner, and also that when the kingbird or the purple martin assails them they must dash into a bush, for it is as impossible to fight the little pests as it is for the fat apple-woman to catch the small boys who have raided her basket. All these things do the young crows know; but they have taken no lessons in egg-hunting yet, for it is not the season. They are unacquainted with clams, and have never tasted horses' eyes, or seen sprouted corn, and they don't know a thing about travel, the greatest educator of all. They did not think of that two months ago, and since then they have thought of it, but have learned to wait till their betters are ready.

September sees a great change in the old crows, too. Their moulting is over. They are now in full feather again and proud of their handsome coats. Their health is again good, and with it their tempers are improved. Even old Silverspot, the strict teacher, becomes quite jolly, and the youngsters, who have long ago learned to respect him, begin really to love him.

He has hammered away at drill, teaching them all the signals and words of command in use, and now it is a pleasure to see them in the early morning.

'*Company 1!*' the old chieftain would cry in crow, and Company 1 would answer with a great clamour.

'*Fly!*' and himself leading them, they would all fly straight forward.

'*Mount!*' and straight upward they turned in a moment.

'*Bunch!*' and they all massed into a dense black flock.

'*Scatter!*' and they spread out like leaves before the wind.

'*Form line!*' and they strung out into the long line of ordinary flight.

'*Descend!*' and they all dropped nearly to the ground.

'*Forage!*' and they alighted and scattered about to feed, while two of the permanent sentries mounted duty – one on a tree to the right, the other on a mound to the far left. A minute or two later Silverspot would cry out, '*A man with a gun!'* The sentries repeated the cry and the company flew at once in open order as quickly as possible towards the trees. Once behind these, they formed line again in safety and returned to the home pines.

Sentry duty is not taken in turn by all the crows, but a certain number whose watchfulness has been often proved are the perpetual sentries, and are expected to watch and forage at the same time. Rather hard on them it seems to us, but it works well and the crow organization is admitted by all birds to be the very best in existence.

Finally, each November sees the troop sail away southward to learn new modes of life, new landmarks and new kinds of food, under the guidance of the ever-wise Silverspot.

III

There is only one time when a crow is a fool, and that is at night. There is only one bird that terrifies the crow, and that is the owl. When, therefore, these come together it is a woeful thing for the sable birds. The distant hoot of an owl after dark is enough to make them withdraw their heads from under their wings, and sit trembling and miserable till morning. In very cold weather the exposure of their faces thus has often resulted in a crow having one or both of his eyes frozen, so that blindness followed and therefore death. There are no hospitals for sick crows.

But with the morning their courage comes again, and arousing themselves they ransack the woods for a mile around till they find that owl, and if they do not kill him they at least worry him half to death and drive him twenty miles away.

In 1893 the crows had come as usual to Castle Frank. I

was walking in these woods a few days afterwards when I chanced upon the track of a rabbit that had been running at full speed over the snow and dodging about among the trees as though pursued. Strange to tell, I could see no track of the pursuer. I followed the trail and presently saw a drop of blood on the snow, and a little farther on found the partly devoured remains of a little brown bunny. What had killed him was a mystery until a careful search showed in the snow a great double-toed track and a beautifully pencilled brown feather. Then all was clear – *a horned owl.* Half an hour later, in passing again by the place, there, in a tree, within ten feet of the bones of his victim, was the fierce-eyed owl himself. The murderer still hung about the scene of his crime. For once circumstantial evidence had not lied. At my approach he gave a guttural '*grrr-oo*' and flew off with low flagging flight to haunt the distant sombre woods.

Two days afterwards, at dawn, there was a great uproar among the crows. I went out early to see, and found some black feathers drifting over the snow. I followed up the wind in the direction from which they came and soon saw the bloody remains of a crow and the great double-toed track which again told me that the murderer was the owl. All around were signs of the struggle, but the fell destroyer was too strong. The poor crow had been dragged from his perch at night, when the darkness had put him at a hopeless disadvantage.

I turned over the remains, and by chance unburied the head – then started with an exclamation of sorrow. Alas! It was the head of old Silverspot. His long life of usefulness to his tribe was over – slain at last by the owl that he had taught so many hundreds of young crows to beware of.

The old nest on the Sugar Loaf is abandoned now. The crows still come in spring-time to Castle Frank, but without their famous leader their numbers are dwindling, and soon they will be seen no more about the old pine-grove in which they and their forefathers had lived and learned for ages.